USA TODAY bestselling author **Janice Maynard** loved books and writing even as a child. After multiple rejections, she finally sold her first manuscript! Since then, she has written fifty-plus books and novellas. Janice lives in Tennessee with her husband, Charles. They love hiking, travelling and family time.

You can connect with Janice at:

janicemaynard.com,
Twitter.com/janicemaynard,
Facebook.com/janicemaynardreaderpage
and
Instagram.com/therealjanicemaynard.

Bombshell for the Black Sheep

JANICE MAYNARD

MILLS & BOON

First published in Great Britain 2019
by Mills & Boon, an imprint of HarperCollins*Publishers*
1 London Bridge Street, London, SE1 9GF

Large Print edition 2019

© 2019 Janice Maynard

ISBN: 978-0-263-08375-0

For Kathy and Patti:

Families are complicated at times—
understatement! Thanks so much
for being the best sisters ever.
Love you both!

One

Hartley Tarleton had made a lot of mistakes in his life, but walking away from Fiona James—twice—had to be the dumbest. He'd had his reasons. Extenuating circumstances. Familial obligations. Still, he'd handled things badly. The woman in question was not likely to be in a conciliatory mood. Even worse, here he was—proverbial hat in hand—to ask for a favor.

Despite a host of misgivings, he parked across the street and a few cars down from her neatly kept bungalow-style home. The middle-class Charleston neighborhood had aged gently, preserving the best of the city's Carolina charm in a price range single people and young families could afford. Fiona was a landscape painter. A very talented one with a quickly burgeoning reputation. Hopefully, her starving-artist years were behind her.

Drumming his fingers on the steering wheel, Hartley rehearsed his speech. The home and the woman drew him, creating a burning ache in his chest. He'd spent two nights in that house, though not in succession. For reasons he wouldn't examine too closely, he recalled every detail.

On difficult days this past year, he had calmed himself by remembering the vintage dinette set in Fiona's tiny breakfast nook. The table was yellow, speckled with gray. He had imagined Fiona, with her naturally curly red hair and wide-set gray-blue eyes, sitting in one of the chairs with the chrome legs, a sketch pad in front of her.

Slowly, he got out of the car and stretched. This momentary procrastination was unlike him. If anything, he erred on the impulsive side. When he was a teenager, people criticized those tendencies as a sign of immaturity. He preferred to think of himself as grabbing the bull by the horns. He liked controlling his own destiny.

A trickle of sweat ran down the center of his back. The day was ridiculously hot and humid. Maybe he had been gone too long. Charleston was his home. Why then, did he feel like an interloper?

His heart hammered in his chest as he crossed the street and walked up the path. He had worried that Fiona might be out and about, but her carefully restored VW Bug sat in the driveway. The car was cotton-candy pink with tiny blue seahorses scattered across the hood. It was a whimsical vehicle, and perfectly suited to the imagination of an artist.

On the porch, he loosened his tie and told himself he wasn't going to lose it. Grief and a host of other emotions bombarded him. His throat was desert dry. Grimly, he reached out and rang the buzzer.

Fiona heard the doorbell and sighed with relief. She had ordered several hundred dollars' worth of new paint—oils and acrylics. The overnight rush fee made her cringe, but it was her own fault for not realizing sooner that she didn't have what she needed to begin a newly commissioned project.

She was wearing a paint-stained T-shirt and ancient jeans with holes in the knees, but the delivery guy had seen her in worse. Her back protested when she sprang to her feet. Sitting in one spot for too long was an occupational hazard. When she was deeply involved in her work, she could paint or draw for hours and never notice the passage of time.

Sprinting through her small house to the front door took a matter of seconds. The only thing that slowed her down was stubbing her toe on the back corner leg of the sofa. *Damn, damn, damn.* The pain had her hopping on one foot. She had to hurry, because the package required a signature.

She flung open the door, breathless and panting, momentarily dazzled by the bright sunshine. The man standing on her porch was definitely not a delivery man. Nor was he a stranger.

It took her a full five seconds to process the unimaginable.

"Hartley?" Her shock quickly changed to

anger. "Oh, heck no." This man had bruised her ego and maybe even broken her heart.

She slammed the door on instinct. Or she *tried* to slam the door. One big foot—clad in a size-twelve Italian leather dress shoe—planted itself at the edge of the door frame. The foot's owner grunted in pain, but he didn't give up his advantage.

"Please, Fiona. I need your help."

There it was. Her weakness. Her Achilles' heel. Growing up in a succession of pleasant but unexceptional foster homes had taught her that becoming indispensable to the family in question secured a roof over her head.

She'd been self-sufficient for over a decade now—ever since she had aged out of the system. She had money in the bank, and her credit rating was unblemished. This perfect little house was almost paid for. Pleasing people was a habit now, not a necessity. A habit she had vowed to break.

But when she actually peeked at Hartley's face, her resolve wavered. "You look terrible," she muttered, still with her hand on the door blocking his entrance. Her statement wasn't entirely correct. Even haggard and with dark smudges of exhaustion beneath his eyes, Hartley Tarleton was the most beautiful man she had ever seen. Muscular shoulders, slim hips and a smile that ought to be outlawed on behalf of women everywhere.

They had first met more than a year ago at the wedding of mutual friends, Hartley a groomsman and Fiona his matching attendant. He had escorted her down the aisle during the ceremony. Later that evening, after a raucous reception that involved copious amounts of extremely good wine and plenty of dancing, he had removed her ghastly fuchsia bridesmaid dress…in her very own bedroom. Where she had invited him to join her.

That night, their physical and emotional connection was immediate and seductive—impossible to resist.

When she woke up the following morning, he was gone.

Today, his coffee-colored eyes—so dark as to be almost black—glittered with strong emotion. "Please, Fee." His voice was hoarse. "Five minutes."

What was it about this man that tore down

every one of her defensive barriers? He'd walked out on her not once, but twice. Was she a masochist? Normally, she didn't fall for stupid male flattery. But she had actually believed Hartley had been as caught up in the magic of their tantalizing attraction as she'd been.

Sighing at her own spineless behavior, she stepped back and opened the door wider. "Fine. But five minutes. Not six. I'm busy."

It was a pitiful pretense of disinterest. When he stepped past her, the familiar crisp, fresh scent of his shave gel took her back to a duet of nights she had tried so desperately to forget.

Hartley crossed the room and sprawled on her sofa. She remained standing, arms folded over her chest. The first time they met, he had worn a tuxedo befitting his inclusion in the wedding party. Nine months later when he had shown up on her doorstep without a word of explanation for his long absence, he'd been in faded jeans and a pale yellow cotton shirt with rolled-up sleeves.

Today, his hand-tailored suit screamed money. Despite his almost palpable misery, he looked like a rich man. In other words, not the sort of person Fiona should date. Or sleep with. Or include in any kinds of future plans.

The silence stretched on. Hartley leaned forward, elbows resting on his knees, head bowed. He was a man who always knew what to say. The kind of guy who could summon a woman's interest with one mischievous, wicked quirk of his eyebrow.

Now that she had let the big, bad wolf into her house, he was mute.

The uninterrupted, empty silence finally broke her. "What do you want, Hartley?"

The five words were supposed to be inflected with impatience and disinterest. Instead, her voice trembled. She winced inwardly, hoping he hadn't noticed. If ever there was a time for a woman to seize control of a situation and play the hand on her terms, this was it.

He didn't deserve her sympathy.

At last, he sat up and faced her, his hands fisted on his thighs. There were hollows in his face that hadn't been there before. Unmistakable grief. "My father is dead," he croaked. The expression in his eyes was a combination of childish bewilderment and dull adult acceptance.

"Oh my God. I'm so sorry." Despite her anger, her heart clenched in sympathy. "Was it sudden?"

"Yes. A stroke."

"Were you in Charleston?" They had discovered at the wedding that they both lived in the beautiful low-country city, but clearly they moved in different circles most of the time.

"No. But it wouldn't have mattered. He was gone in an instant."

"I don't know what to say, except that I'm very sorry, Hartley."

"He was old but not *that* old. It never occurred to me I wouldn't get the chance to say goodbye."

She wanted to sit down beside him and hug him, but she knew her own limits. It was best to keep a safe distance. Sliding into Hartley Tarleton's arms made her reasoning skills turn to mush.

His jaw firmed. "I need you to go to the funeral with me. Please." He stood and faced her. "I wouldn't ask if it weren't so important." The muscles in his throat flexed as he swallowed. He needed a haircut. When one thick lock fell over his forehead, he brushed it aside impatiently.

She had seen him naked. Had felt the gentle caress of his big, slightly rough hands on every inch of her sensitive skin. That other Hartley made her body sing with pleasure...made her stupid, romantic heart weave daydreams. But she didn't know him. Not really.

"I don't think it's a good idea, Hartley. We're nothing to each other. You made that abundantly clear. I don't *want* to go with you to the funeral," she said firmly, trying to sound tough and no-nonsense and not at all like the type of woman who let a man disappear for days and weeks on end with no explanation and then three months ago took him back into her bed...again.

"You don't understand." He moved a step in her direction, but she held him off with a palm-out stance.

"No touching," she said, reading his playbook. She wouldn't let him soften her up.

He shrugged, his expression harried. "Fine. No touching. But I need you to go to the funeral with me, because I'm scared, dammit. I haven't seen my brother or sister in over a year.

Things have been strained between us. I need a buffer."

"Charming," she drawled. "That's what a woman wants to hear."

"For God's sake, don't be difficult, Fee."

His scowl would have been comical if his behavior hadn't been so atrocious. "*I'm* perfectly reasonable and rational, Mr. Tarleton. You're the one who seems to have lost your mind."

He ran a hand across the back of his neck, a shadow crossing his face. "Maybe I have," he muttered. He paced restlessly, pausing to pick up a nautilus shell a friend had brought her from Australia. It had been sliced—like a hamburger bun—with a fine-gauge jeweler's saw to reveal the logarithmic spiral inside. Hartley traced the pattern with a fingertip, the gesture almost sensual. "This is beautiful," he said.

"I just brought it out of my studio. I've been working on a series of four watercolors…a galaxy, a hurricane, this perfect shell. The pattern occurs in nature more often than you might think."

He closed his palm around the opalescent wonder and shot her a look. "And the fourth?"

Her face heated. "Oddly enough, it's a kind of broccoli… Romanesco."

For the first time, the tension in his broad shoulders eased visibly, and a trace of his trademark grin lightened his face. "I've never met anyone like you, Fiona."

She bristled. "What does that mean?"

"You're special. You see the world in a way us mere mortals don't. I envy you that."

The quiet sincerity in his voice and the genuine compliment reminded her of all the reasons she had fallen for his charms the first time. And the second. His habitual smile was an inexplicable combination of sweet and sexy. For a man who stood six three in his stocking feet and carried himself like an athlete, the hint of boyish candor caught her off guard again and again.

What could it hurt if she accompanied him to his father's service? It was an hour of her life, maybe less. She sighed inwardly, already losing the battle. "What day is the funeral?"

Now he definitely looked guilty. "Today."

She gaped at him. "*Today* today?"

"In an hour and a half."

Her temper ramped to a slow boil. "And you

seriously thought you could simply waltz in here, demand my cooperation and get what you want?"

"No," he said forcefully. "No." The second denial was quieter. "I was *hoping*, Fee. Just hoping."

He shoved his hands in his pockets, and he didn't move. She gave him points for that. Everything in her past interactions with him suggested that he could indeed get what he wanted with little more than a kiss. But Hartley didn't try any funny business. All he did was ask.

Before she could formulate an answer, he grimaced. "I know I owe you explanations for my behavior. If you'll do me the kindness of standing beside me this afternoon, I swear I'll tell you whatever you want to know afterward. I won't run out. Not this time."

She searched his face for the truth. "Why are things awkward with your siblings? Isn't your brother your twin? I seem to recall you telling me that. Aren't twins supposed to be tight?"

"I did something to upset my father and Jonathan, my brother. I was written out of the will. And to be honest, maybe I deserved it. But I love my family. They're everything to me. I would like to heal the rift…if that's even possible."

He could have wheedled. Or flirted. Or even pressured. Instead, he simply stood there. Looking at her. So intently that her nipples tightened beneath the soft cotton of her bra. She hadn't imagined the physical connection between them. It was as real today as it was the other times he had blasted into her world. As real as the mantel clock that ticked a steady rhythm.

"Okay. I'll go with you." A platonic date to a funeral didn't mean she was capitulating a *third time.* "I can be ready in half an hour. Will that do?"

He nodded. "Thank you, Fiona." His gaze was sober. "I appreciate it."

"Wait for me here. If the doorbell rings, please answer it. I'm expecting some packages."

Hartley watched her walk away, wishing he could join her in the shower and forget that his life was imploding. It was nothing short of a miracle that she had agreed to go with him. Because of the situation he was in and the looming stress of seeing his family again, he had to slam the lid on all the erotic memories this small house contained.

His gut was in a knot, but the burning dread eased. With Fee beside him, he could get through this afternoon.

Before he could pull out his phone and check his email, a loud knock sounded at the door. The uniformed delivery man on the porch was beaming when Hartley answered the summons, but his smile faded.

"I have some packages," he said.

Hartley didn't call him out on the awkward, unnecessary explanation. "I see that," he said mildly.

The kid, barely twenty at most, tried to peer inside the house. "Fiona needs to sign for this delivery."

Hartley's territorial instincts kicked in. "*Ms. James* is in the shower."

The young man recognized the veiled rebuke. His face flushed. "You could do it, I suppose."

"I supposed I could." Hartley scrawled his name and handed back the electronic clipboard. "I'll tell her you said hello."

Three large boxes changed hands. Hartley gave the poor schmuck a terse nod and closed the door firmly. He couldn't blame the kid for having a crush, but Fiona deserved a man in her life.

The irony of that didn't escape him. In fact, now that he had Fee in his corner, he could spare a moment to wonder what she had been up to in the weeks and months he had been traveling the world. Was there a man somewhere who would protest Hartley's current involvement in her life?

His stomach-curling distaste for that thought told him he was more invested than he wanted to admit. It seemed impossible he could be obsessed with a woman he had known for less than a week, collectively. Yet of all the people in his life who could have been persuaded to accompany him to his father's funeral, Hartley had chosen Fiona.

The momentary peace he experienced deep in his heart told him he had made the right decision.

A lot of things were going to change in the next weeks and months. Even if his brother didn't trust him and his sister would reproach him for being gone so long, the three of them would have to work together to settle their father's affairs.

Only Hartley knew how very difficult that was going to be.

A noise in the hall brought his head up. His breath caught in his throat. "Fiona," he croaked. "You look amazing."

Her classic black dress was sleeveless and knee length. Sexy black sandals showcased slender legs. She had tried to tame her medium-length hair with two antique tortoiseshell combs. Now fiery curls framed her elfin face. "Is this okay?" she asked. "To be honest, I haven't been to a funeral in a very long time." She toyed with the simple pearl earrings that matched the necklace at her throat.

"You're perfect," he said.

Two

Fiona avoided funerals on a good day. Attending this particular one on the arm of the man who had treated her so shabbily didn't make sense.

Yet here she was.

Charleston, in all her low-country charm, basked in the summer sun. The city was a unique amalgam of Southern gentility and a lingering painful past. Palm trees and horse-drawn carriages. Elegant secluded courtyards. And everywhere, the patina of old money. Farther out from the city, pockets of poverty existed, but here in the historic district, wealth and social position held sway.

By the time Fiona and Hartley made it to the upscale funeral home in the heart of town, she knew she was in trouble. Hartley had barely spoken a word the entire time, but she was hyperaware of him at her side.

He drove with careless confidence despite the tightness in his jaw and his palpable air of tension.

It was impossible not to think about the other times they had been together. At least it was impossible for *her*. Presumably, Hartley was too distraught to think about sex.

She was having second and third thoughts about her role this afternoon. "So what do I need to know?" she asked. "I don't want to say anything I shouldn't."

Hartley shot her a sideways glance before spotting an empty spot down the street and parallel parking with ease. "Just follow my lead. My sister will be emotional. For several reasons. She doesn't know why I've been gone."

"Join the club," Fiona muttered.

Hartley ignored her sarcasm. "Mazie's husband is J.B. He's been a friend of ours since we were kids. He and Mazie reconnected recently and fell in love. And to further confuse you, J.B. is my brother's best friend."

"Got it."

"Jonathan, my twin, had serious brain surgery not too long ago, but he's made a complete recovery. His wife is Lisette. She's been working for Tarleton Shipping a long time."

"And your mother? I haven't heard you speak of her." Fiona got out and smoothed her skirt with damp hands. Meeting strangers was not her forte. In this situation, the stakes were much higher than usual. Hartley got out as well and closed his door, resting his arms on the roof of the car as he stared at her. "My mother is not in the picture. The only people you'll have to deal with today are my siblings and their spouses."

If his words were meant to reassure her, they failed. Hartley's air of mystery told her the Tarleton family had more than one skeleton in the closet. Why else would Hartley be so worried about seeing his brother and sister? It was beginning to dawn on Fiona that his brief though startling contact with her was not the only relationship he had abandoned.

They arrived at the funeral home early. Hartley wanted time to speak with his family before the receiving of friends began. When he took Fiona's hand in his as they mounted the steps to the red-brick and white-columned building, she wasn't sure he even noticed.

She tugged him to a halt before he opened the door, squeezing his fingers, trying to extend her support. "It's going to be okay," she said softly. "Every family goes through this. You'll make it. You all will."

His expression was grim. "Death is one thing. Handling the living is something else again."

His odd words stayed with her for the next half hour, illuminating the awkward family reunion.

Mazie was the first person to spot her brother. She ran up to him and threw her arms around his neck, her face wet with tears. "I swear I shouldn't forgive you, but I'm so glad you're here."

Fiona hung back as Hartley embraced his classically beautiful sister. Mazie's skin was fairer than her brother's. And though the family resemblance was strong, her eyes were more golden amber than brown. Her elegance made Fiona feel dowdy in comparison. Mazie wore emeralds that must have cost a fortune.

Hartley reached back and drew Fiona into the small circle. "Mazie, this is my friend, Fiona James. She was kind enough to be my date today."

Fiona grimaced. "I told him no one needs an escort to a funeral, but he wouldn't take no for an answer."

Mazie smiled through her tears. "That sounds like Hartley. Wait a minute," she said. "Fiona James the artist? My husband and I have a couple of your paintings. *The Salt Marsh at Sunset. The Bridge at Twilight.* I treasure them. You're incredibly talented."

"Thank you," Fiona said. It still startled her to be recognized.

Mazie dried her face with a tissue. "Jonathan is just around the corner. You might as well get this meeting over with."

Hartley's gaze darkened. "Is he really going to be okay?"

"Right as rain," Mazie said. "He didn't even freak out when Lisette told him she had been keeping you in the loop. Apparently, staring death in the face mellows a man."

Hartley curled an arm around Fiona's waist. "Jonathan was misdiagnosed in the beginning, but fortunately, the mistake was caught in time."

"How scary," Fiona said.

Mazie nodded. "Terrifying. We thought we were going to lose him."

They turned down a hallway and more or less ran into the third Tarleton sibling. Jonathan had clearly overheard the end of their conversation.

He lifted a shoulder, his smile laconic. "Apparently, I'm hard to kill."

The two brothers sized each other up. The tension was painful. They were definitely identical twins. No hiding that. But even an outsider would have no problem telling them apart.

Olive skin. Dark brown eyes. Chestnut hair. Those were the commonalities. Hartley's hair was longer...untamed...sun-bleached. And he had the look of a man who spent a lot of time outdoors. Jonathan, on the other hand, was *GQ* handsome. Sculpted jaw. Expensive haircut. Conservative suit.

Two stunningly handsome men in their prime.

Hartley kept an arm around Fiona's waist. "Hello, Jonathan."

Mazie made a huffing noise. "For God's sake. Hug each other."

The brothers ignored her. At last, Jonathan held out his hand. "Welcome home, Hartley."

Even without being privy to all the details, Fiona knew this moment was epic. It was written in Jonathan Tarleton's wary expression and in the rigid set of Hartley's posture.

"Thank you," Hartley said quietly. "I'm glad to be back, but not for this reason. I'm sorry I wasn't here when it happened."

Mazie spoke up, her tears flowing again. "None of us were. Apparently, he died in his sleep. The housekeeper found him."

"Hell," Hartley said quietly. "I knew he wasn't well, but I honestly thought he would go on forever."

"So did we." Jonathan glanced at his watch. "Would you like to see him?"

Fiona felt the shudder that racked Hartley's body. "Yes," he said gruffly.

Moments later, the four of them stood around the casket. Gerald Tarleton had been a large man. But in death, he looked old and frail. Fiona knew he had built a far-reaching shipping empire that would now pass on to his children. Again, she wondered about Mrs. Tarleton. Was she dead or alive?

Soon they were joined by J.B. Vaughan and Lisette, Jonathan's wife. Mazie took care of the introductions. Her husband wrapped her in his arms and kissed the top of her head. "No more crying, honey. You'll give yourself a migraine." He dabbed his wife's cheeks with a handkerchief.

Fiona felt a fierce stab of envy. Would any man ever look at her with such naked devotion?

Her stomach curled with tension. Dozens of floral arrangements flanked the casket and filled the walls on either side. The heavy scent of carnations made Fiona feel ill. A cold sweat dampened her brow.

Could she leave? Could she simply run away? This wasn't *her* family crisis. Suddenly, she knew she needed a moment to gather her composure. But before she could make a break for it, the funeral home director appeared behind them and intruded with a hushed cough.

"Guests are arriving," he said, his tone sepulchral. "If you'll follow me, I'll escort you to an anteroom. We'll open the doors, and then I'll bring you in and arrange the receiving line."

This was Fiona's chance. In the transition, she darted down the hall and found the ladies' room. Once in the stall, she retched and dry-heaved. Oh, God. She felt terrible. Her life was usually placid and peaceful. She *liked* it that way. Damn Hartley for pulling her into the middle of this mess.

When the crisis passed, she put a cold paper towel on the back of her neck and touched up her makeup. All her life she had never done well with confrontation and stress. Lack of stability in her formative years had left her with issues. Duh.

Her psyche craved calm, the kind of steady, peaceful existence her art gave her. She was happiest when she could lose herself in a creative project. Seeing Hartley again and having to negotiate his family storms made her a nervous wreck.

Still, he said he *needed* her. That had been enough to coax her into accompanying him during this difficult afternoon. She'd spent too many years ingratiating herself with different foster families to change her personality overnight.

She was independent now. She didn't have to

worry about housing or food or even winning a kind word from a stranger. But the desire to fit in...to be useful...was never far from the surface.

Fortunately, the crowds of visitors had already overtaken the room where the Tarleton family stood to greet friends and business acquaintances. Fiona was able to slip in unnoticed and take her place at Hartley's side. He gave her a quick intimate glance, but immediately returned his attention to the seemingly endless line of men and women waiting to speak to him.

Fiona smiled and nodded, content to remain in the background. Occasionally, someone questioned Hartley about his long absence from Charleston. Each well-meaning query was deflected with a vague throwaway comment.

The man was a social genius, even if he did have more disappearing acts than Houdini.

At last, it was time to adjourn to the chapel. A couple of songs, some readings and a few words from Jonathan. Finally, it was over.

Fiona couldn't wait to leave. Her stomach still felt iffy, and her head ached. Before she could plan her exit, Mazie appeared at her side.

The other woman's eyes were red-rimmed, but she was calm. "A few of our friends have catered a dinner for us out at the beach house. We'll be headed that way in a few moments. Don't let Hartley escape."

"Oh, no," Fiona said. "This is your family time. I need to go home. It was lovely to meet you."

Mazie frowned and strong-armed Fiona into a nearby corner. "Please, Fiona. You don't know all the details." She paused and grimaced. "To be honest, I don't even know. But Jonathan and Hartley had a huge falling-out about something, something big. This is the first time they've been in the same room in over a year. They *have* to heal this thing. And we need you to be an impartial bystander."

"Why?" Fiona asked, searching desperately for a polite way to make her excuses.

Mazie's eyes filled with tears again, though this time perhaps not for her father's passing. "I adore my brothers. They've been my supporters and protectors my entire life. It kills me to see them so stiff and polite with each other. *Please*, Fiona," she said urgently. "Please have dinner with us."

Hartley walked up to them, overhearing his sister's invitation. "Of course she's coming—right, Fee?"

Fiona knew she was trapped. She gnawed her lip. "If you're sure I won't be intruding." She gave Hartley a pointed stare. "But I can't stay too late. I have a huge project to begin tomorrow, and I want to be in bed at a decent hour."

His gaze was inscrutable. "Understood."

Hartley was no more communicative during the drive to the Tarleton home than he had been earlier en route to the funeral. The silence suited Fiona just fine. She leaned her head back against her seat and closed her eyes.

Unfortunately, shutting Hartley out was not so easy. His masculine scent teased her nose. Her fingers itched to cross the divide between them and stroke his thigh. She *wanted* to help him. She really did. And she wanted to be with him. But her sense of self-preservation warned her to keep her distance.

Instead, she was accompanying him to a meal and a social occasion that was sure to produce strong emotions and any one of a dozen possible outcomes, from uncomfortable silence to vocal recriminations.

If she was lucky, the Tarletons would be on their best behavior. Fiona would be able to return home and would never again answer her door to a tall, handsome lover.

Despite her misgivings, she was eager to see the beach house. Years ago, Gerald Tarleton had built a walled compound on the tip of a barrier island north of Charleston. Fiona knew of the property in general terms, but when Hartley steered the car through the front gates, she was both taken aback and enchanted.

The structure rested on massive stilts, of course. A sweeping staircase led up to the beautiful double-door entrance. Even from the driveway, Fiona could see the intricate stained glass that incorporated sea turtles, dolphins and starfish. As an artist, she was fascinated.

As a woman, she wanted to run far away.

Hartley shut off the engine and pressed the heels of his hands to his forehead. "This feels so damned wrong."

"I'm sorry." The words were inadequate, but she didn't know how else to help him.

The early evening light illuminated his drawn expression. "I grew up here," he said quietly.

"After 9/11, our father was paranoid. He barely let us leave the house for the longest time."

"I can understand that, I suppose. He wanted to protect you." She gazed up at Hartley's family home. It was a far cry from the houses where she had been bounced around.

Her longest tenure was twenty-five months—with a family who had taken in four other foster children besides Fiona. When the wife eventually became pregnant with her own *biological* child, Fiona and her de facto brothers and sisters were reassigned.

Fiona had begged to stay. At thirteen, she was the oldest of the lot and capable of being a help around the house. But the pregnancy was high risk. The doctor said too much stress and chaos would threaten the mother's health.

Fiona's personality was quiet and self-abnegating. No chaos anywhere. But the doctor's orders prevailed.

Fiona's foster mom had cried and cried. She was too hormonal and stressed out to make a good decision. In the end, it was nobody's fault, but Fiona had never again invested so much of herself emotionally.

Hartley touched her hand. "Ready to go inside?"

Even that one quick brush of his fingers against her skin sent shivers dancing down her spine. Why did he have this effect on her? "Shouldn't I be asking *you* that question?"

His low laugh held little humor. "My brother and I are civilized people. You don't have to worry about fistfights."

"I wasn't," she said. "Until now."

Her attempt at humor took some of the darkness from his face. "C'mon," he said. "You'll like the house."

Fiona's sandals had spiky heels, so she didn't protest when Hartley held her elbow as they ascended the stairs. His touch made her knees weak. She had missed him...so very much.

She tried to remember how angry she was about his cavalier treatment of their budding relationship. But the bitterness of his absence winnowed away in the pleasure of having him near again. It was sobering to admit she was perilously close to letting bygones be bygones.

Though it was frustrating not to be able to resist his winsome charm, she liked the woman she was with him. He made her feel sensual and desirable.

Before Hartley was forced to make a decision about letting himself in or ringing the bell, Lisette opened the door and greeted them. Fiona wondered if that was deliberate, so his siblings wouldn't be in the position of welcoming him back to his own home.

"Everyone is gathered in the dining room," Lisette said. "The food looks amazing. There's enough for half a dozen families."

When the six adults were settled around the table, the housekeeper began setting out the meal on the antique sideboard. The food had come from a top-notch restaurant in the city. Fresh seafood. Ribs. Roasted corn on the cob. The dishes were endless.

The meal and the accompanying conversation progressed in fits and starts. During one awkward pause as wineglasses were being refilled, Hartley leaned in and spoke softly to Fiona. "My siblings are both still relatively new to this marriage gig. Mazie moved in with J.B. after the wedding. Jonathan and Lisette are building their own place." His warm breath brushed her ear, making her shiver. The arm he curled across the back of her chair hemmed her in intimately.

Jonathan overheard the quiet exchange and lifted an eyebrow. "You're curiously well-informed for a prodigal son."

The edge in his voice was apparent.

Hartley shrugged with a lazy smile. "I have my spies."

Fiona forced herself to wade in. Someone needed to defuse the rising tension. "What will happen to the beach house?"

Three

Nobody said a word. As Hartley watched, Fiona's face turned bright red. There was no way to avoid land mines with *this* family around the table. To her, it must have seemed like an innocuous question.

Jonathan spoke up, his smile careful but kind. "It's a little early to be thinking about those decisions. This was our father's fortress, his safe place. He didn't ever tell me what he wanted to do with the house when he was gone, and I didn't ask. I'm sure the lawyers will guide us through probate."

Suddenly, Hartley had reached his limit. They were all on their best behavior because of the funeral, but one thing was certain. Jonathan wasn't opening his arms to let Hartley back into the fold. The unspoken message was clear. Hartley had walked away, and true forgiveness was in short supply.

He stood abruptly. "It was good to see you all. Thanks for the meal. I'd like to take Fiona for a walk on the beach, and then we'll head out."

Mazie looked stricken. "Are you leaving town again?"

Again, that awkward silence.

Hartley shook his head slowly. "No. I'm back for good." There was so much he wanted to explain...so many family secrets to unravel. But how could he upend his siblings' lives for no other reason than to justify his own behavior? It wasn't fair to anyone. Maybe he would *never* tell them.

Fiona stood as well. "It was lovely to meet all of you. Sorry it was not under better circumstances."

Moments later, the ordeal was over.

Outside in the driveway, Hartley looked down at Fiona's shoes. "You can't walk in those on the beach."

"Barefoot is fine." She slipped off her sandals

and tossed them in the car, adding her small clutch purse as well.

Hartley removed his jacket, tie, shoes and socks, feeling as if he were peeling away layers of frustration and grief. He had always loved the beach, and this house in particular. "The ground is rough between here and the gate," he said. "Get on my back, and I'll carry you to the sand."

Fiona looked at him askance. "I can walk."

He ground his jaw. "It's a piggyback ride, not foreplay."

"Don't get snippy with me, Hartley. I'm not the enemy."

She was right. He couldn't let Fiona bear the brunt of his mood. "Sorry," he muttered. "Climb on."

He watched as she shimmied her skirt up her thighs. Maybe he was wrong about the foreplay. Fiona's legs were enough to keep a man awake at night. When she moved behind him, he hitched her up on his back and curled his hands beneath her warm, supple thighs.

Fortunately for his self-control, the path beneath the house and out to the gate was not far. Fee reached around him to disengage the lock, and soon they were at the water's edge. He let her slide off his back slowly, steadying her with one hand as she stumbled.

There was no moon. The water seemed dark and menacing. But the whoosh and roar of the waves was a familiar lullaby from his childhood.

He tried to empty his mind of all the sorrow and confusion that had consumed him since he heard the news that his father was dead. Gradually, the inexorable pattern of the tide soothed him.

Fiona stood at his side in silence, her presence both a comfort and a niggling frustration. Twice now, he had made love to her and walked away. The first time, he'd had no choice. The second, he'd been reluctant to embroil her in his family drama. Maybe he sensed that he was using Fiona as a crutch. Maybe he hadn't wanted to let her get inside his head. In both instances, his behavior was logical if not particularly admirable. But what was going to happen moving forward?

If he still wanted to sleep with Fee, and he did, most emphatically, then he needed not only her absolution, but also some notion of what was ahead for him professionally. Anything beyond that was more than he wanted to contemplate right now.

Almost as if she had read his mind, Fiona spoke softly. "What do you do for a living, Hartley? We've flirted and slept together, but I don't really know much about you at all."

Her question prodded an unseen wound. He cleared his throat. "Well, before I left Charleston for an extended period, I was a full partner in Tarleton Shipping. We were working on a proposal to add a boatbuilding arm...pleasure craft. That whole deal was going to be my baby."

"And now?"

He shrugged. "I doubt my brother has any interest in working with me after everything that has happened."

"Because of this mysterious *falling-out*?"

"Yeah." He sighed. "Jonathan is one of the finest men I've ever known. A straight arrow all the way. But as alike as we are physically, our personalities don't always mesh."

"Why did you not live at the beach house?"

"I got tired of butting heads with my father over the business. Jonathan had a knack for handling him with kid gloves. Dad and I only yelled at each other. Several years ago I bought an investment property at a premier golf community north of the city. I was the one who would wine and dine clients. Play a few rounds with them on the course. I liked being outdoors, even if golf wasn't really my thing. But I closed deals and grew the business."

"Who has done that while you've been gone?"

It was a simple question. Not meant to inflict pain. But it hit at the heart of his guilt. "I don't know." Fiona hadn't been the only one he hurt when he'd hared off to Europe. He'd left behind his family and the shipping business and cut all contact. He'd had his reasons. In retrospect, though, he honestly didn't know if he'd done the right thing.

Fiona moved restlessly. "The beach is lovely, Hartley. I really do need to get home, though."

"I promised you explanations. It's late. I don't suppose I could sleep on your sofa?" He threw it out there hopefully. Fiona's little house represented the peace and comfort he had lost in this last year.

"No," she said bluntly. Without another word,

she started up the beach toward the gate in the high brick wall.

"Fair enough." He loped up the incline and scooped her into his arms. It was a tougher slog through the loose sand this way, but he persevered. He needed to hold her.

Fiona didn't fight him. As soon as they were back at the car, though, she insisted on wriggling out of his embrace. After smoothing her hair and brushing the sand from her feet, she put on her sexy sandals.

Then she stood, hands on her hips, and watched him re-dress. "You don't owe me explanations. I told you that."

He rounded the car and cupped her face in his hands. Lightly. Gently. "I *want* to tell you, Fee. And in the spirit of honesty, I'd like to sleep with you again."

"Sleep?"

She had him there. "Sex," he muttered. Even to his own ears, he sounded like a jerk. But he wouldn't dress it up. He couldn't offer her anything more. His life was total chaos. Besides, Fiona would demand full-on honesty and intimacy from any man who shared her life for the long haul. That wasn't him.

Her expression was mutinous. In the glow of the security light, the stubborn tilt to her chin was obvious. "*Sex isn't the answer to all your problems*, Hartley."

"Maybe not, but it would be damned good, and if you're honest, you'll agree. I know I messed up. I won't do that to you again."

"How can I believe you?" Her low laugh held a hint of dismay. "It's a painful cliché, but I'm a kid who came through the foster system. Never got adopted. I have a few abandonment issues. Your recent behavior hasn't helped."

How many women would have the guts to be so vulnerable? He had a lot to answer for and no clear idea how to fix the messes he had created. "I want to kiss you, Fee," he muttered. "But I'm trying my damnedest to respect your boundaries."

Tears glittered in her eyelashes. She sniffed. "Shut up and do it, you aggravating man."

It was all the invitation he needed. He wanted to snatch her up and take everything she had to give. Instead, he kissed her coaxingly, softly. Trying to tell her without words how much he regretted his missteps.

Fiona made a choked little noise in her throat

and finally kissed him back. When her slender arms curled around his neck, he felt as if he had won the lottery. She was soft and perfect against his chest. He lifted her off her feet, desperate to make the kiss last.

"I'm sorry," he muttered. "So sorry I hurt you."

"You're forgiven. Doesn't mean I'm a glutton for punishment." She pushed away from him after a few seconds. Reluctantly, he let her go.

"So, what now?" he asked quietly.

"Nothing. At least not today. Or even tomorrow. *Twice*, I let you talk your way into my bed like I was a sixteen-year-old girl with her first crush. That was *my* mistake. I make no guarantees, Hartley. None."

He rolled his shoulders, realizing ruefully that he had been a little unrealistic about where this evening might lead. Even if he'd been saying all the right things, apparently his libido had jumped ahead to more titillating scenarios. "Understood," he sighed.

He started the engine and waited for her to climb into the front seat. The ocean breeze had tousled her hair. It stood up around her head

like a nimbus, making her a weary goddess…
or a naughty nymph.

Which did he want? The angel or the sexy
sprite? In his imagination, she was both.

He turned the radio on for the drive back to
Charleston. As they pulled away from his father's home, Hartley glanced in the rearview
mirror. Jonathan stood at the top of the stairs,
his arms folded across his chest.

Seeing his brother tonight had been surpris-
ingly painful. After all this time, Hartley had
been hoping Jonathan might have relented…
that he had come to know instinctively that
Hartley would never do anything to bring harm
to his family.

But apparently, some hurts ran deep. Jonathan wasn't wiping the slate clean. In fact, he
hadn't made any mention of the future at all.
Hartley was on his own.

When they reached Fiona's street, she gathered her purse and started to climb out as soon
as the car rolled to a halt. He took her wrist.
"Wait, Fee. Please."

Her body language was wary. "What?"

"Let me take you to lunch tomorrow. I'll tell
you the whole story, start to finish." He needed

to tell *someone*. The secrets were gutting him. But his family was off-limits until he decided whether or not the truth would be too damaging. Fiona was a neutral player.

"I have to work tomorrow," she said.

"Dinner, then?" He was close to begging on his knees.

She hesitated for far too long. "Fine. But if this story is as convoluted as it seems, we should eat at my house. I'll fix spaghetti."

"I want to treat you," he said.

"You can't spill salacious secrets in the middle of a crowded restaurant. Besides, this isn't a date, Hartley. You seem to have a need to bare your soul, and I've agreed to listen. That's all."

"You're a hard woman."

"It's about time, don't you think?"

"I remember what it's like to make love to you, Fee. You can't blame a guy for wanting to re-create the magic."

"The magic is gone. You killed it."

Her words were harsh, but she was still sitting in his car. He took that as a good sign. "I love spaghetti," he said. "What time?"

"Six o'clock. Don't assume you'll be able to

coax me into letting you spend the night. That's off the table."

"Yes, ma'am. You're cute when you're busting my balls."

"Grow up, Hartley. I'm immune to you now."

I'm immune to you now. Fiona had never told a bigger lie in her life. She slept poorly and woke up the following morning disturbed by the vivid dreams that had plagued her. Being with Hartley again kindled a hunger in her belly that no homemade spaghetti was going to fill. She wanted him. Still. After everything he had done. It was a shocking realization.

Despite her unsettled mood, she was a professional artist. That meant working regular hours even when her muse had taken a hike. Today was a case in point. It was harder than it should have been to concentrate on her new project… three massive panels that would hang in one of the main rooms of Charleston's visitor center.

Commissions like this one were her bread and butter. They paid the light bill and kept food in the fridge. But they weren't humdrum. Never that. She poured her heart and soul into every brushstroke.

Because of the size of the canvases, she'd had to buy a special easel that held the work in progress secure. At certain moments, she would have to stand on a ladder to complete the highest portions. Her sketch—the one the city had approved—included historical images all the way from Charleston's founding up until modern times.

A giant undulating current swept through the center of each panel, propelling the milestones of progress from decade to decade. Included in the visual telling were some very painful periods in time. She could see the finished product in her mind. The challenge she faced was being able to successfully translate her vision into reality.

It was her habit to paint for a couple of hours when she first awoke and then take a break for coffee and a light brunch. After that, she would typically labor for another five or six hours and quit for the day. Hard work and determination had brought her to this place in her career. She was conscious that her success was based on a great many things beyond her control, so she was determined to make the most of her current success.

This morning, though, she found herself swamped with inexplicable fatigue and a draining lethargy that forced her to go in search of calories after only forty-five minutes in her studio.

In the kitchen, an unexpected déjà vu brought her up short. She and Hartley had stood in this very spot and made bacon and eggs amidst much laughter and many hot, hungry kisses.

She put a hand to her chest, trying to still the flutters of anxiety. Hartley wouldn't force her to do anything she didn't want to do. Her problem was far closer to home. It was *her*. Fiona. The woman with the deep-seated need for love and acceptance.

Hartley made her happy, but more than that, he made her wish and dream, and *that* was dangerous.

The fact that she had slept with him twice was no big deal. They'd had fun. Their sexual chemistry was off the charts. He was smart and kind and amusing, and she had never met a more appealing man.

But it was the long view that worried her. Like the deadly undertow out at the beach, Hartley had the power to drag her under...to tear apart the life she had built for herself. She was proud of her independence. She didn't lean on any man for support.

The danger lay in the fact that without even trying, he made her want to throw caution to the wind. When she was with him—and also when she wasn't—the smart, careful, cautious side of her brain shut down.

Even now, all she could think about was how much she wanted to share a bed with him again. Naked and wanton. Losing herself in the elemental rush of sexual desire. Hartley made her *alive*. And she loved it.

But with great joy came the potential for great heartbreak.

With the way she was feeling, it was too much trouble to cook anything. Instead, she opted for cereal and a banana. A cup of hot tea warmed her cold fingers. When she was done with breakfast, she carried a second serving of tea to the living room and curled up on the couch.

Cradling the china cup in her hands, she debated calling off tonight's dinner. Who was she kidding? If Hartley came over, she would sleep with him. Wouldn't she? Did she have it in her to say no?

Sitting here alone, it was easy to see all the problems.

The Tarletons were Charleston royalty. They and J.B.'s family, the Vaughans, had endowed libraries and funded hospital wings and sat on the boards of half a dozen philanthropic organizations across the city. Their bloodlines went back to pre–civil war times.

Fiona appreciated her own worth, but she was a pragmatist. Hartley appeared to have the attention span of a moth. He was interested in Fiona at the moment, because his life was in crisis. And because they had shared a couple of encounters that had all the earmarks of a romantic comedy.

Life wasn't like that, though. In the long run, the chances that he would actually come to love Fiona were slim. Maybe she was his flavor of the month right now, but when the novelty paled, he would be off on another adventure, with another woman, and Fiona might be left with a broken heart if she were foolish enough to fall for him.

Despite all her hashing and rehashing of the

facts, she couldn't bring herself to text him and say *don't come*. How pathetic was that? She desperately wanted to see him. And then, of course, there was her curiosity about where he had been all these months.

He had never struck her as a liar. If he had explanations to make today, she had a hunch they would be true. Fantastical maybe, but true.

She finished her tea and stood, only to have the room whirl drunkenly.

With a little gasp, she reached behind her for the arm of the sofa and sat down gingerly. Had she poured bad milk in her cereal? Her stomach flipped and flopped. What was going on?

Five minutes later, she tried again. This time the familiar outlines of her furniture stayed put, but the nausea grew worse. At the last moment, she made a dash for the bathroom and threw up, emptying her stomach again and again until she was so weak she could barely stagger to her bedroom.

She curled up in the center of the mattress, shaking and woozy, and pulled the edge of the comforter over her.

Then it hit her. A possibility that had never once crossed her mind…though it should have.

Was she pregnant? She'd had these odd episodes for several weeks now...had written them off as a virus or inner ear trouble or low blood sugar.

Her heart hammered in her chest. Her periods were not regular...never had been. At her gynecologist's urging, Fiona typically noted them on a paper calendar she kept in the bedside table.

When she thought she could move without barfing, she reached for the drawer, extracted what she needed and stared numbly at the unmarked boxes. Back one month. Then two. Then three. At last, she found it. A brief notation in her own handwriting. She'd had her period about ten days before Hartley last showed up at her house.

Dear Lord.

He'd used protection. Hadn't even balked at the idea when she told him she wasn't on the pill. In fact, he'd used protection that night after the wedding, too. He'd been a generous, thoughtful lover.

But no method of birth control was 100 hundred percent. And now that she thought about it, three months ago, they had made love multiple times during the night when they were both half-asleep. Had they messed up? Was there one of those times when his body had claimed hers skin to skin?

Her teeth started to chatter. She couldn't tell him. Not yet. Not until she was sure. He was going to be at her house in a few hours. With a moan of mortification, she buried her face in the pillow.

Yet even as she trembled with fear, excitement and happiness bloomed in her chest. A baby? Was she really pregnant? This could be the future she had always dreamed of...the family she so desperately wanted.

Hartley didn't have to be involved, but he *had* to be told.

Four

Hartley felt like a sailboat with a broken mast. He was home to stay. His time away had always been temporary. But his siblings hadn't known that, because he hadn't told them.

He'd left Charleston in order to be a hero. To fix things. And he'd succeeded in part. All the answers to all the questions had been found, thanks to his extended visit in Europe. Ironically, those answers were too dangerous and painful to explain to Jonathan and Mazie.

Had it all been worth it? Or had he ruined his relationships for nothing? On the day after his father's funeral, he found himself going in circles, or at the very least, becalmed.

What was he going to do with himself? If Jonathan wasn't keen or willing to have him back at Tarleton Shipping, Hartley was lost.

His enormous home adjacent to the world-class golf resort was not *him*. Never had been. At least that was one thing he could change. He spent the day taking care of small maintenance issues, and then called a Realtor and set up an appointment for the following morning.

He was going to sell his house. Immediately.

Maybe he would rent something in Fiona's neighborhood while he figured out his next step. She couldn't help him revamp his life—that was up to him—but sharing her bed would keep him sane. If she allowed it.

By the time four thirty rolled around, he was hot and sweaty but feeling pretty damn good about himself. He jumped in the shower, humming with more enthusiasm than expertise. With the prospect of seeing Fiona tonight, he had plenty of reasons to be upbeat.

His life had taken some unexpected turns, but he would get himself back on course. His siblings were all he had. Fiona was an alluring distraction from his painful family situation. Maybe it was wrong to pursue her. Maybe it was cowardly. Because if he used her and walked away again, he knew in his gut the damage would be permanent.

It would be smarter and kinder to stay away.

Even so, at ten till six, he pulled up in front of her charming home, grabbed the gifts he had brought and locked the car. He thought he saw the edge of a curtain twitch, but maybe not.

When he knocked, she answered almost immediately. "Hi, Hartley. You're right on time." She was wearing a daffodil-yellow sundress that bared her shoulders and emphasized her modest breasts.

He kissed her cheek. "These are for you."

She glanced at the label of his three-hundred-dollar bottle of wine and raised an eyebrow. "A little over-the-top for homemade spaghetti, don't you think? What if we save it for a special occasion? I made iced tea. And there's beer in the fridge…the kind you like."

He was ridiculously pleased that she remembered his preferences. A tiny detail, but a good sign…he hoped. "Sounds like a plan," he said. "Shall I put the flowers in water?" He'd brought her yellow and white roses, a summery bouquet that suited her home and her personality.

"Yes…thanks. You'll find a vase underneath the sink."

The conversation was stilted for two people who had seen each other naked. He wanted to say to hell with dinner and take her straight to the bedroom. "Did you have a good day painting?"

She whirled around, her eyes wide. "Why do you ask that?"

He cocked his head. "You told me you're starting a big new project."

"Oh." She flushed, her gaze skating away from his. "It was fine. Beginnings are always hard."

"Are you okay, Fee?" Now that he thought about it, she seemed pale…and nervous. She hadn't been this skittish the first afternoon they met. At that endless wedding rehearsal.

"Of course I'm okay." Her voice was muffled, because she had stuck her head and shoulders halfway into the fridge.

He glanced at the stove. "Do I need to turn off the heat? The spaghetti is boiling over."

"Oh, damn." She whirled around and rescued the pasta just in time.

He put his hands on her shoulders. "Fiona. Take a breath."

She shrugged out of his grip and put her hands to her cheeks. "Sorry," she muttered. "I'm a little nervous about having you here."

There it was again. That raw honesty. He winced. "I can go. If that's what you want."

They stared at each other across the small kitchen. "No," she said at last. "I don't want you to go."

Thank God. He reached for her hand and linked his fingers with hers. "I swear I'll be on my best behavior."

At last, she smiled at him. It was wobbly, but it was a smile. "I find that highly unlikely." She rested her head against his shoulder. "I'm glad you're here. Really, Hartley. I am."

His hands trembled with the urge to touch her. Coming here was wrong. He knew it. But he couldn't walk away from her a third time. Even if all they had was sexual chemistry, he wanted to erase his past transgressions. He needed to prove he could be trusted.

"Well, that makes two of us," he said heartily. "Now, tell me how I can help with dinner..."

* * *

Fiona was embarrassed and relieved at the same time. Hartley had taken her behavior in stride, it seemed. They consumed the simple meal and shared innocuous conversation without incident. Though she felt as if her secret was written on her face, she was clearly overreacting. There was no way for him to know the truth.

She had to get a grip.

"Let's go to the living room," she said when they had cleared the table and loaded the dishwasher side by side. "If you're going to bare your soul, I want a comfy spot."

Hartley followed her, chuckling. "I never promised that."

She curled up on a chair that was only big enough for one. No point in tempting fate. "You don't have to do this," she said.

Hartley shrugged. "You're the perfect listener. A disinterested bystander."

Fiona's heart sank. That wasn't what she wanted to hear at all. Hartley hadn't come to her tonight as a trusted confidante. She was about to be his therapist or his shrink. The distinction was painful.

She swallowed her hurt pride and reminded herself that Hartley wasn't her Prince Charming. Never would be. "Start at the beginning," she said.

Now he was the one to look uncomfortable. Maybe he hadn't rehearsed what he was going to say. "Well…"

"I'll refresh your memory," she offered helpfully. "After the wedding, I invited you here to my house. We both knew what was going to happen. It *happened* three times that night, and when I woke up, you were gone."

"Geez, Fiona. You make it sound so sleazy." He paced restlessly.

"How would you describe it?"

"I had airline reservations for the morning after the wedding. I was supposed to be on a flight out of Charleston at 7 a.m. You were a complication I never expected. I didn't know how to explain."

"Ah."

"It's true," he said.

She stared at him soberly. "Where were you going?"

"London first. I met with a private investigator who used to work for Interpol."

Fiona wrinkled her nose. "I think you've left out some pertinent details. Why would you need a PI?"

Hartley hunched his shoulders, his expression bleak. "Two days before the wedding, I received a blackmail note."

"Seriously?" Her skepticism was warranted, surely.

"The letter threatened to go public with a painful Tarleton family secret if I didn't give the blackmailer a million dollars."

"Hartley. This sounds like a spy novel."

"What you don't know is that my mother has been living in an inpatient mental health facility in Vermont since my siblings and I were preteens. A few people in Charleston know the truth, but not many."

"So you decided to do what?"

"My father's health was failing. Jonathan had been working his ass off at Tarleton Shipping, trying to keep the business afloat. My sister spent her adolescence without a mother. Our family has suffered more than our share of hard times. I didn't want the gossip."

"Everybody knows you can't pay off a blackmailer. Surely you didn't."

"Of course not. But I needed the money in hand just in case. I wasn't sure what else this mystery person might be willing to do. And I didn't know why we were targets."

"What did Jonathan say?"

Hartley's neck flushed. "I didn't tell him. I thought I could handle everything on my own. In retrospect, that wasn't too smart."

"I have to agree. Did you have a million dollars lying around in the bank?"

"Not exactly. I've told you about Jonathan. He's a play-by-the-book kind of guy. Never cut corners. Never bend the rules. If I had told him why I needed the money, he would have asked a ton of questions and then shut me down. I couldn't take that chance."

Her eyes widened. "What did you do, Hartley?"

He shrugged. "I took the money out of our account at work. It wasn't stealing. I own a quarter of the business."

"But you didn't tell Jonathan what was going on."

Hartley heard the criticism in her statement. "No. Like I said, he was under a lot of stress. I wanted to handle this grenade and defuse it. I never imagined that my brother and my father would jump to the absolute worst conclusion."

She shook her head slowly. "That's a lot to ask, Hartley. Blind faith?"

"They know me. Why would I take the money if not for a damned good reason?" It still pissed him off that he'd immediately been painted the villain. Even worse, it *hurt*.

"Secrets backfire all the time." Fiona's expression was wry. "I can't say that I blame them, Hartley. You didn't trust them enough to believe you could all work together. Surely you see that was a mistake."

Maybe he did now. With the benefit of hindsight. "Well, I can't undo the damage, so it's a moot point."

"Mazie seems to have forgiven you."

"That's only because Dad and Jonathan kept her in the dark. If she knew the truth, she'd probably give me the cold shoulder, too."

"Let's circle back. So you took the money, and you went to London. What next?"

"Eventually, I tracked the letter back to a small village in Switzerland. The blackmailer was a relative on my mother's side. Her uncle, to be exact."

"Why would he want to hurt your family?"

"That's what I needed to know. As it turned out, he was only trying to get my attention. The letter he sent me served its purpose. It got me to Switzerland. Uncle Hans had fallen on hard times. An extended illness had wiped out his savings. He was in danger of losing his house and his dairy farm."

"Did you turn him over to the authorities?"

"How could I? He was a sick man in his late seventies. Frail. No family left. I felt I owed him something."

"So you *did* give him money."

"I paid off his house and put some cash in his bank account. Not much at all by our standards, but he was grateful and it made me feel better. I barely put a dent in the million. I ended up staying with Hans for a couple of months, filling in the blanks. He had a lot of stuff like family Bibles and heirlooms…things he wanted me to see. Items to pass on."

Fiona frowned. "There's something you're not telling me. Why did you come back to Charleston three months ago? And then leave again?"

"I came back to talk to my father and my siblings about why I had been gone. I had information they needed to know. But I chickened out at the last minute. Revealing everything I had learned in Europe was a potential bomb that threatened to blow up in my face. You were the only person I saw or spoke to. After that night in your bed, I went back to Switzerland to pack up my things."

"And then what?"

He shrugged, his eyes bleak with remembrance. "The uncle passed away. Rather suddenly. I found myself in the odd position of having to settle his meager estate."

"Even then, you didn't talk to your family?"

"I couldn't. The conversation was something that needed to be handled face-to-face. But with Hans gone, I began to ask myself if it wouldn't be better to keep everything I had learned to myself."

"What was this terrible secret, Hartley?"

His jaw was carved in stone, his profile no longer the affable man she had come to know. "The woman in that facility in Vermont—the woman who no longer recognizes us because she had a complete breakdown—the woman who is the only mother we've ever known—is *not* our mother."

Fiona couldn't sit still any longer. She jumped to her feet and went to him. Wrapping her arms around his waist, she rested her cheek against his chest, inhaling the pleasant laundry scent of his crisp cotton shirt. "That doesn't even make sense."

He eluded her embrace and continued to wear tracks in her rug. "Apparently, when my siblings and I were toddlers, my father took our mother to Switzerland to visit her family. She hadn't been back since they were married. They left us kids behind in Charleston with a trusted babysitter."

"Okay…" Her mind raced ahead, trying to guess the outcome. But nothing clicked into place.

Hartley's body language was agitated. "According to Hans, my mother committed suicide when they were in Switzerland. Apparently, she had been planning it for some time. There was a note. Hans still had it in the Bible. In her mind, it was better to do the deed where no one in Charleston would know. Maybe she thought my father would invent an accident. Hell, I don't know. She was a very sick woman."

"But I don't understand. Who is living in Vermont?"

He stopped his pacing and faced her. "My *aunt*. My mother's twin sister."

"Good Lord..." Her mind reeled.

"According to Hans, after my mother died, my aunt volunteered to marry my father, return to the States with him and step in as our mother."

"But surely someone would have noticed."

"I told you my father kept the family hidden away. Now all the security and the secrecy make a lot more sense. Maybe he was afraid. He knew keeping the business afloat was all up to him. Maybe he thought being a father was more than he could handle. Or maybe he was so distraught with grief, he wasn't rational."

"It's hard to believe..."

"Hans had pictures of the two women side by side. The sisters were identical. Any household staff here in South Carolina were vetted carefully. And maybe we kids were too young to know the difference."

"I don't know what to say."

"Pardon me for being flip, but being a foster kid doesn't sound so bad now, does it?"

She knew his angry sarcasm wasn't directed at her. "So you're telling me your father lost not one but two wives to mental illness?"

"Yes. And it also makes more sense, I suppose, that he sent the second Mrs. Tarleton so far away when she began to show signs that she might hurt herself or one of us. She wasn't the woman he loved. That tragedy—losing the love of his life—had happened long ago."

"The poor man."

"It's a lot to comprehend. Things were different back then. My father was much older than my mother. I don't think he would have ever considered raising us on his own. He would have been in shock when the suicide happened. Why did my aunt volunteer to take on a ready-made family? Perhaps her life in Switzerland was unhappy. We'll never know, because none of us can get through to her."

Fiona sank onto the sofa, her mind whirling with Hartley's story. Definitely a case of truth being stranger than fiction. "How long were you there after your uncle died?"

"About eight weeks. I sold the house and the

farm and settled all the outstanding accounts. I had already shipped several boxes of memorabilia back to the States. I assumed Mazie would be interested one day, even if Jonathan wasn't. All I could think about was coming home, talking to my father, asking him a million questions. And then I got Lisette's phone call. Dad was gone. Now all his secrets are buried with him."

"You *have* to tell Mazie and Jonathan. You have to, Hartley."

He turned and stared at her, his face carefully blank. "I don't know that I do, Fee. I think the kinder thing is to leave well enough alone."

Five

Hartley felt empty…wrung out. Tonight—with Fiona—was the first chance he'd had to work through all of this. Hearing himself say the words aloud settled something in his gut.

He sat down beside her, his body limp with resignation and grief. Without overthinking it, he took her hand in his. Her nails were neatly trimmed but unpolished. Her fingers had calluses in certain spots. She might be small in stature, but she was tough in mind and body. Soft and sensual in bed. A force to be reckoned with when the sun came up.

"Think about it," he said, rubbing her palm with his thumb. "My siblings and I already knew our DNA carried the possibility of mental illness. But *two* sisters in the same family? Twins? That ups our chances of passing on whatever genetic anomaly took our mother from us. The medical community has made huge advances in treatment, but there are no guarantees."

"Isn't that all the more reason to warn them?"

He shook his head. "Mazie and J.B. have been battling infertility already. They may end up adopting. Lisette had a tragic miscarriage only weeks after their wedding and another one two months later. I assume they're trying again, but who knows? I can't be the one who makes those decisions for them. I won't play God. If I tell them what I know, it could change the entire course of their relationships."

"And what about you?" Fiona was milk pale. His story had upset her more than he had anticipated.

"I won't have children," he said bluntly. "All the secrets. All the lies? Families are supposed to love and support each other. I've paid the price for my father's failings. I won't put an innocent child through that."

Her eyes glistened with tears. "Don't you

think your brother and sister and their spouses deserve that same clarity?"

He cursed beneath his breath, feeling put upon from all sides. If he'd been able to talk this over with his father, maybe he could have made the right decision. Now all he had were doubts and uncertainties.

"Don't push, Fee. I've been to hell and back. What do you want from me, damn it?"

She stood up slowly, her expression impossible to decipher. "So have I, Hartley. But life goes on. You've had a terrible day...a terrible year. Come to bed with me."

He jerked back, caught between exultation and the absolute certainty that it would be a mistake to sleep with her right now. "I don't need your pity," he muttered. "I'll go."

"Forget the past," she whispered. "Forget the wedding weekend when we met and the night we had after the reception. Forget the moments you spent in this house three months ago. Forget the funeral and the fact that your family is shutting you out. None of that matters right now. I want you, and I think you need me. Let's take tonight for ourselves."

Something about her urgent speech bothered

him. Below the surface there was faulty reasoning in the words. But he was finally where he wanted to be, and she was offering him the chance for redemption.

He wasn't a saint—far from it. It was an invitation no mortal man could resist. Fiona. After all these lonely, terrible weeks.

"I came here for dinner, Fee. Nothing more. I swear."

Her smile was wistful. "I think we're both good at kidding ourselves. I can't explain this thing between us other than to call it elemental attraction. You said you wanted to have sex with me again. Maybe what we need is a chance to say goodbye and to have closure."

"Closure?" He mouthed the word with distaste, vaguely alarmed that she was giving him the brush-off in the midst of seducing him.

"I have two huge projects ahead of me," she said. "You have a lot of decisions to make about your life and your relationship with your family. If you're honest, being with me has been an escape for you, nothing more. Your life is one big train wreck right now. I forgive you. I'm not playing games."

He had a choice. He could stand here and

argue with her about the future, or he could take what she was offering. In the end, emotional exhaustion won out. He needed her. He wanted her.

She was so beautiful it made his chest ache. Her pale, creamy skin was dotted with the occasional freckle. Those wide-set eyes were a combination of smoke and the sea. The wildness of her fire-kissed hair struck a marked contrast to the serenity she projected.

No woman had ever affected him so immediately, so deeply. Something about her made him want to make love to her and bask in her peaceful spirit at the same time.

He felt cold inside. Fiona promised him warmth.

"Fine," he said. "Call it whatever you want. I won't say no to you. Not tonight."

She took his hand. He let her pull him to his feet. He was charmed and pleased that she was taking the initiative. In their earlier encounters he'd been the aggressor, the coaxer. Now, his sweet Fiona was staking a claim.

In her bedroom, they faced each other with odd hesitance. They had been virtual strangers before. Things were more *real* now.

"Should we check the doors?" he asked. "Set the alarm?"

She cocked her head. "The doors are locked. I don't have an alarm."

He frowned. "I don't like that. I'll buy you a new system. You need one."

"Hartley…"

"Hmm?"

"Shut up and kiss me. Before I change my mind."

"Yes, ma'am."

Three months. It had been three long months since he tasted her. The memories paled. She melted into his arms, stealing the breath from his lungs. Every part of him hard and taut with wanting. "I've missed you," he said huskily, nipping her lower lip with his teeth, sliding his tongue over hers. "So damn much. I used to lie in bed at night and calculate the distance between Switzerland and South Carolina."

Fiona wrapped her arms around his neck. "At least you knew where I was. All I had were a million questions. Actually, until you showed up on my doorstep three months ago, I didn't know if you were alive or dead. That sucked, Hartley. A lot."

"I'm sorry." His fingers fumbled with the zipper at the back of her bodice. "I'll make it up to you."

"See that you do."

Her teasing smile lit a fire in his gut. He sucked in a sharp breath when he realized that all she wore underneath the sundress was a pair of simple cotton undies. White. Unadorned.

No silk and lace confection could have been more titillating. He let the dress pool at her feet. "Damn, you're gorgeous."

"My boobs aren't very big."

The hint of uncertainty in her gaze brought tenderness into the mix. He kissed her nose. "They're perfect," he said. Carefully, he cupped her curves in his hands, teasing the pert tips with his thumbs.

Fiona's eyelids fluttered shut. She made a sound that was halfway between a purr and a moan. His erection flexed a centimeter more. "Look at me, darlin'. I want you to watch."

His big, tanned hands were dark against her white body. She sucked in a breath, but she obeyed. "I'll watch," she vowed. "It's my turn now." She unbuttoned his shirt and yanked it from his pants. "Get rid of this, big guy."

Sexual urgency told him to take and take until they were both satisfied. But tonight, he wanted to play another tune. Tonight, he wanted to convince her that he wasn't a bad guy. That there was more to him than the lover who ducked out in the night. Hartley Tarleton wanted to make a good impression.

Unfortunately, his patience for having her undress him was eroding rapidly. "I'll do the rest," he said, kicking off his shoes and bouncing on one foot and then the other as he removed his socks.

Fiona—naked but for panties and a smile—watched as he unfastened his belt and pants and shucked them to his ankles. When he lost his balance and nearly fell on his ass, she had the audacity to giggle.

"The man I remember was smoother than you," she said.

"Maybe I'm nervous," he deadpanned. She didn't have to know it wasn't a joke.

"Hurry up, Hartley. I'm getting cold."

It was still eighty degrees outside, even at this hour. And the AC system in Fiona's little house wasn't all that efficient. Perhaps she was nervous, too. She flipped back the simple yellow-

and-blue quilt and climbed under the sheets. When she reclined on one elbow and crooked her finger, he was toast.

He was completely naked now. Unable to hide his need even if he had wanted to. Fee stared at his bobbing sex and licked her lips. The reaction didn't seem to be intentional. Her eyes had glazed over, and her chest was flushed.

When he made it under the covers and twined his body with hers in a skin-to-skin hug that fried his synapses, Fiona buried her face in his neck. "You are an impossible man, but Lord knows, you're magnificent. I love touching you." She ran her hands over his back and buttocks as if to make a point.

He found it hard to breathe. "Knock yourself out, Fee." She was warm and supple in his embrace. Her enthusiasm for his body made him glad he was a man. He would die happy if all he had to do was let her experiment with his various appendages.

She pulled back so she could kiss his collarbone. "I'm not even going to ask how many women you slept with while you were abroad."

"Not a one," he wheezed, trying not to come like an untested teenager.

When she zeroed in on the spot that was most eager for her attention, his vision went fuzzy. The sensation of her slender, warm fingers wrapped around his sex was indescribable.

She stroked him up and down, slowly enough to make his forehead damp and his muscles rigid. "I find that difficult to believe."

Was she torturing him on purpose? "I may have walked out on you, Fee, but I've never lied to you. After we met at the wedding, I've been too busy to look at other women."

Fiona wanted so badly to believe him, but she'd been a naive fool twice. Was he playing on her sympathies? Did it really matter tonight? He was here...in her bed. Very much alive. His masculinity was raw and erotic in the midst of her ultra feminine bed. The artist in her wanted to sketch him as he sprawled on his back and watched her.

The woman simply *wanted*. Period.

She reclined beside him and ran her hand from his throat to his hip. Warm golden skin was lightly dusted with just the right amount of hair. He was like a beautiful god, at the height of his physical perfection.

At the moment, her stomach was cooperating, thank heavens. Her earlier fears seemed ludicrous. Of course she wasn't pregnant. A woman would know something like that, right? She couldn't possibly be thirteen weeks along and have survived in blissful ignorance all this time.

Still, the possibility filled her with both anxiety and amazement. A child? A baby with Hartley's big brown eyes? An infant who would possess the best and worst of both of them?

Tremors came to life deep inside her body and spread outward. She struggled with waves of fear and exultation and sexual arousal. How could she want this man so damn much when he had hurt her twice and had said recently—with perfect clarity—that he was *never* going to have children?

"Do you have a condom?" she asked, feeling her face heat. Hopefully, he would attribute her red-faced mortification to maidenly sexual frenzy. Until she knew for sure about the baby, she wouldn't take chances.

His gaze narrowed. A feral masculine smile accompanied his terse nod. "One second, darlin'." He leaned over the edge of the bed, giving her a stunning view of his tight butt. "Got it," he said triumphantly, brandishing his wallet.

While he was busy tossing the packet on the bedside table, Fiona raked his ass with her fingernails. The soft fuzz was golden, lighter than the hair on his head, as if he might have sunbathed in the nude while he was in Europe.

Thinking of Hartley naked on a beach somewhere made her dizzy. "I'm glad you came back," she whispered. "I missed you, Hartley."

At her words, his expression softened. "And I missed you, sweet Fiona." He moved between her legs and readied himself. "I don't even care if this is pity sex. I've been dreaming about you in my bed for weeks."

When he pushed steadily, filling her, driving himself home until she winced, it was as if everything in her world righted itself for a moment. And then she understood why. This was their pattern, their sexual MO. One frantic, unable-to-wait-a-second-longer coupling followed by a series of languid, self-indulgent second acts.

Hartley was a big man. Everywhere. Her body accepted his eagerly, straining to make the connection last. His urgency was flattering, his attention to detail admirable. Even as he took his own pleasure, he remembered every erogenous zone he had discovered during their earlier encounters.

A nip at her earlobe. A gentle grinding of his pelvis against hers, putting pressure where she needed it to climb even higher. Her breath caught in her throat. A wave of emotion staggered her, making her weak and weepy. He was so dear. So perfect for her. But he *wasn't* hers, and now he never would be. She had to remember that. Had to keep her heart out of this. Sex only.

She'd always heard people say that pregnant women were insatiable when it came to sex. Was that why she was already thinking about round two? Or was this wild urgency all for Hartley and no other reason?

He went still, his body rigid and trembling. "Fee? Are you with me?"

Her mental distraction hadn't gone unnoticed. "I'm here," she whispered. "Don't stop."

He took her at her word. Reaching between their linked bodies, he caressed the aching center of her need and sent her over the edge. The orgasm was off the charts. Incredible. Mildly astonishing.

The ripples went on and on.

Hartley chuckled hoarsely, wheezing as he attempted to speak while balanced on a sexual precipice. "You make a man feel damn good, Fiona. I'd like to spend the whole night reclaiming lost time. We've wasted months."

She smiled lazily, in an expansive, forgiving mood now that he had satiated her considerable needs for the moment. "*We?* Don't blame this one on me, Mr. Tarleton. I've been right here all along. You're the one who went missing."

His smile sent her buzzing again. "You can punish me later."

He withdrew almost completely and then went faster. Groaning, he thrust rapidly until he hit the peak, shuddering and panting in her embrace until he slumped on top of her, his body warm and damp.

She wrapped her arms around him, feeling his heart pound against her breast. As wrung out as he was, she could almost believe he'd been celibate since the last time they were together.

That was dangerous thinking. Such an idea

made their brief dalliance more than it was. Why would a man avoid sex for the sake of two isolated one-night stands?

Believing in rainbows, pots of gold, unicorns and happily-ever-afters wasn't who Fiona was anymore. Over the course of her adolescence, she had stomped on her rose-colored glasses. She now viewed the world as it was. Broken. Hurtful. Uncaring.

Maybe that was harsh. She had wonderful friends. But the belief that a man and a woman could form a lasting bond on the basis of a few nights of hot sexual insanity was a fiction she couldn't embrace. She wouldn't.

Idly, she stroked the back of his head, feeling the silky hair slide between her fingers. The other Tarleton twin was a fine figure of a man, but she preferred Hartley's rough-around-the-edges masculinity. He could be brash and unrepentant and frustratingly stubborn, but he tugged at her heartstrings as no other man ever had.

When he could breathe again, he lifted his head. "Damn, woman. You're killing me." He kissed her slow and deep, his tongue mating with hers. "I don't want closure, Fee. I want you."

He punctuated his declaration with a string of kisses down the side of her neck, to her throat, to her breasts. Licking them. Nibbling. Forcing her to acknowledge his mastery of her body.

How could he do it to her so quickly? She was on the verge of climax again. Panic gripped her in a choke hold. This had to stop. Her mornings were iffy now. She and Hartley couldn't be wrapped in each other's arms when the sun came up. "You should go," she said, blurting out the words with no finesse at all. "It's late." *I can't take the risk you'll stay until morning, see me barf and guess the truth.*

Six

Hartley jerked, stunned. He would have been less shocked if she had slapped his face. He'd been within an inch of giving his sweet Fee a second orgasm when she slammed some kind of door between them.

He gaped. "Are you serious?" Her raspberry nipples were puckered, begging for his attention.

For some reason, Fiona's gaze slid away. "I have to work early in the morning." She slipped out of bed and tugged the coverlet from the foot of the mattress, wrapping it around herself toga-style. "Thank you for telling me why you were gone so long. I hope you and your brother work things out between you."

He staggered to his feet, his brain racing to understand what had just happened. "Are you angry with me?" He frowned, knowing she had every right to evict him, and yet hurt that she could seem so unaffected by what for him had been cataclysmic.

As he reached for his clothes and reluctantly dressed, Fiona shook her head slowly. Smoky blue eyes stared at him. "Of course not. You did what you had to do."

"The past is the past," he muttered. "I'm more interested in what comes next. I'm not done with you, Fee."

Her eyes flashed. "It's not up to you, now is it? I didn't put my life on hold while you were gone. You can't drop back in and expect everything to be the way you want it."

Was this some kind of test? Was he supposed to work for absolution?

Screw that. He owed her an apology, and he had given it, sincerely and wholeheartedly. But he wouldn't crawl. First Jonathan and now Fiona. Was there no one who believed in him?

When he was fully clad, he shot her an angry

glare. "I get it," he said. "You don't want to sleep with me anymore. Casual sex isn't your thing, is that it? No worries. Now that I'm home for good, I'm sure there are plenty of available women in Charleston. Good night, Fiona. I'll let myself out."

Even then he thought she might relent. She certainly *seemed* miserable. But she didn't say a word as he stormed out. He heard the *snick* of the dead bolt on the front door after it closed behind him. By the time he reached the sidewalk and headed for his car, the lights inside the house had been extinguished. He stood in the middle of the street...all alone.

In a year and a month and a week that had sucked big time, this was perhaps his lowest point. The investigation was over. Fiona no longer wanted him around. He had reconciled with his family...barely. But there was apparently no longer a spot for him at Tarleton Shipping. That ship had sailed.

He couldn't even laugh at his own stupid joke. Nor could he face returning to the house that wasn't a home, the house he was going to sell sooner than later.

Instead, he drove aimlessly around Fiona's

neighborhood. All her fellow Charlestonians were tucked in for the evening. No teenagers on skateboards. No sweethearts kissing good-night on street corners. Just peace and silence and the sense of a community at rest.

And then he spotted it. A small for-sale sign in front of a three-story brick monstrosity. The house was older than its neighbors and in bad need of repair.

Hartley pulled out his phone and looked up the specs on the Realtor's website. From the pictures, it was no wonder the house had been on the market over a hundred days. It probably had dry rot. Black mold. Maybe even termite infestation.

His spirits lifted. It was exactly the kind of project a man needed when he was looking for an anchor. And it had the added advantage of being under his lover's nose.

If he had genuinely thought Fiona was not in-terested in a sexual relationship with him, he would have walked away. After all, they had almost nothing in common beyond a visceral attraction. But *she* was the one who invited *him* to her bed tonight. Because the sex was great.

Right? Up until that very last part, she had been a willing and eager participant.

It was a puzzle. One he was happy to study until he found the answers. For now, he would give her some space.

Unfortunately, not even a real estate agent hungry for a sale would appreciate a call after eleven at night. Hartley would have to be patient until morning. He decided to make a lowball cash offer, and then while he tried to woo his prickly artist, he would have a project to keep him busy.

Having a plan brought a measure of resolve. He hated uncertainty...always had. Make a choice, even if it's the wrong one. That's how he operated.

It was late. He knew he needed to go home. But there was one more sore spot he needed to explore.

From Fiona's house, the drive to Tarleton headquarters took no time at all. The building was as familiar to him as his childhood bedroom. He parked right in front. Nothing to hide. Inside, there would be a night watchman somewhere.

At the main entrance, he entered a six-digit

code in the electronic keypad and swiped his ID card. To his surprise, the door opened easily. Had Jonathan forgotten to revoke his credentials? Or had he believed Hartley would eventually come home? Either way, it soothed some of Hartley's rough-edged discontent to know he was able to walk inside.

His desk and his office were exactly as he had left them. For the first time, he began to understand how difficult his absence must have been for Jonathan. The questions. The work piling up.

A sound in the outer office had him whirling on his heel. Jonathan leaned against the wall, his expression inscrutable. Clearly, he had gone home after work and come back, because he was wearing old jeans and a T-shirt that had seen better days.

Hartley felt his neck heat. "I was just looking around. I wasn't here to steal the silver."

Jonathan shrugged. "I'm not accusing you of anything."

"Not at the moment." Hartley grimaced. Being at odds with his twin was a physical pain. He cleared his throat. "I'll go. Sorry to have bothered you."

Jonathan held up a hand. "You put the money back yesterday." It was neither a simple statement nor a question, but maybe a blend of both.

"I did, yes."

"Why?"

"I was *always* going to put it back. But neither you nor Dad cared to ask for an explanation. You just assumed the worst."

His brother frowned. "Don't turn this on me. *You* were the one who made off with a million bucks as if it were nothing more than Monopoly money."

"I had my reasons."

"Okay." Jonathan folded his arms across his chest. "Let's hear them. I've got all night."

It was a challenge. Plain and simple. A showdown. But Hartley was going to have to swallow his pride and walk away. He'd already told the story once.

No matter how much he wanted to erase the gaping void between him and his brother, he couldn't dump what he knew on Jonathan. Not without thinking it through.

Maybe Fiona was right. Maybe he owed his siblings the truth. But at what cost? They would both be hurt, as Hartley had been. Unsettled.

Dismayed. And without their father to provide answers, this information Hartley had uncovered served no useful purpose.

Hartley cleared his throat. "It's late. The tale will keep for now. Good night, Jonathan."

When he went to slip past the president and CEO of Tarleton Shipping, his brother put a hand on his shoulder. For a moment, they both breathed the same air. Jonathan squeezed briefly, then stepped aside. "I believe you had your reasons. They may not have been good reasons. I'd still like to hear them."

Jonathan was reaching out. Making the first move. Being the bigger man.

Hartley was frozen with indecision. The irony of the situation would have been humorous if the stakes hadn't been so high. Here he was, a guy who believed in always stepping out, sure the path would appear from within the fog.

Now, when it mattered the most, he couldn't do it. The truth had hurt Hartley badly. Why inflict that pain on the man who shared his blood? The brother he loved.

He swallowed hard. "My reasons don't exist anymore. That's why I put the money back. I'm sorry I left you hanging, though. You've carried the brunt of Father's illness and the way that complicated the business. I'm sorry, Jonathan. I really am."

His brother's smile was wry but genuine. "You'd do the same thing again, though. Am I right?"

Hartley considered the question. Ignorance might be bliss, but not for him. He'd done what he had to do to protect his family. Maybe his ultimate task was to be the keeper of the secrets.

"Yes," he muttered. "I'd do it again. Why didn't you tell Mazie about the money?"

Jonathan raked a hand through his short hair, for the first time, betraying exhaustion. He looked beaten. Defeated. "Mazie adores you. I didn't know where you were or why you were gone. The missing money only made it worse. I figured you deserved whatever happened to you, but Mazie's big heart would have been shattered."

"Thank you," Hartley said.

"Don't thank me. I did it for her."

The snap in Jonathan's voice was both startling and depressing. Hartley's twin might have made an overture a few moments ago, but he was still very angry.

Nothing was going to be gained by rehashing old arguments. The untold truth lay between them, terrible and dangerous. It had unmanned Hartley, left him despairing and aching with hurt. Although it had been cathartic to unburden himself to Fiona, he hadn't even let her hear the worst of it. Unless Hartley was willing to tell Jonathan what had transpired in Europe, there was nothing left to say.

"I'll let myself out," he said dully. "Good night."

The morning after Hartley made love to her, Fiona knew without a doubt that she had made the right choice in sending him home. She awoke violently sick, unable to hold down either tea or toast until almost noon. Then, it was all she could do to drag herself to the studio.

She needed to buy a pregnancy test. That was how these situations worked. The thought of getting in a car and driving somewhere was more than she could manage.

So she painted. In short bursts of energy. Twenty minutes here. Thirty minutes here. Astonishingly, the project began to take shape. By late afternoon, she actually felt hungry.

She was cleaning brushes and tidying her work space when her doorbell rang. *Hartley.* Was she irritated by his persistence or flattered that he was back again?

When she opened the door with a neutral smile, the smile faded. Her caller wasn't Hartley. Instead, Mazie Tarleton Vaughan stood on the porch. "May I come in?" she asked, not bothering with social niceties like hellos or explanations.

"Umm…" Fiona felt awkwardly self-conscious, as if Mazie could see the possible pregnancy on her face.

The other woman vibrated with impatience. "I won't stay long."

There was nothing more to say after that, short of being unforgivably rude. "Of course…" Fiona stepped back, allowing her unexpected visitor to enter.

Hartley's sister surveyed the small house, at least the parts she could see from the foyer. "This is nice," she said. "It suits you."

"Thank you, I—"

Mazie interrupted. "We can do the get-to-know-you thing another day, but I'm here to talk about Hartley. Is he okay?"

"What do you mean?" Fiona winced inwardly. She had never been good at prevarication.

"Don't play dumb…please. My own brother has kept me in the dark. I don't need it from you, too. Hartley has a thing for you. Obviously. Which means he must have told you why he left. Right?"

Suddenly, Fiona could see beneath Mazie's imperious demand to the scared sister underneath. "Why don't we sit down?" She steered her guest toward the comfortable sofa and perched on the armchair that had seen better days. "I do know some of it," she said carefully. "But only very recently did he tell me anything. I was as much in the dark as you were. Yes, he's fine. A little lost maybe…after being gone so long."

"He needs to be back at Tarleton Shipping. He belongs there."

"I'm not sure he feels welcome."

Mazie's eyes widened. "What do you mean?"

"Your brothers have some issues to work out. According to Hartley, Jonathan is angry. And not inclined to welcome the prodigal with open arms."

Mazie burst into tears.

Well, crap. Fiona was not equipped to deal with all this family drama. It was why she lived alone. And worked alone. Still, she was not hard-hearted enough to ignore the other woman's distress.

She sat down beside Hartley's sister and handed her a tissue. "It will work itself out. Give them time."

Mazie wiped her eyes and sniffed. "You clearly don't know my brothers very well. They are both stubborn as sin."

"Well, based on the one I *do* know, I have to agree."

Tears continued to roll down Mazie's cheeks. Somehow, Hartley's sister was as beautiful as ever. Hardly seemed fair. When Fiona cried, her face turned into a blotchy mess.

Mazie sniffed and scrubbed her cheeks with her hands. "Don't mind me. I've been on fertility drugs, and I'm a mess."

"That must be stressful," Fiona said quietly, keenly aware that her own body was out of her control at the moment. "Is there anything I can do for you? A cup of hot tea, maybe? I'm a bit of a connoisseur. Tea always helps me when it's that time of the month, so I keep plenty of bags on hand. I can offer you a wide range of choices."

Hartley's sister sat up straight, an arrested look on her face. She grabbed up her purse, took out her phone and opened a calendar app. "Oh, wow."

"What is it? What's wrong?"

"I've been so upset with the funeral and everything that I haven't paid attention."

"Paid attention to what?"

Mazie's expression was equal parts wonderment and bewilderment. "I missed my period, Fiona. I'm six days late."

Seven

Fiona smiled. "That's good, right?"

Her visitor was pale, her chin wobbly. "We've been disappointed so many times. I can't tell J.B. Not yet." She grabbed Fiona's arm. "Will you do me a favor?"

"Well, I—"

"Nothing big. Everybody in this city knows my family. If I stop in somewhere and buy a pregnancy test, word will get back to my husband before I return home. I don't want to get his hopes up until I know for sure."

Fiona felt like she was in the middle of a bad joke. "You want me to buy you a pregnancy test?"

Mazie's smile was sunny and cajoling, her tears forgotten. "Please. I'll drive. All you have to do is run inside the store and get it for me. Easy peasy."

"How can I say no?" Fiona wanted to laugh, but she didn't dare. "Let me change clothes. I'm speedy. Won't take long."

In her bedroom, she stripped off her jeans and T-shirt and stared at herself in the mirror. At this particular moment, she didn't *feel* pregnant. Her tummy was flat, her body unchanged. Maybe she had the flu. The summer flu that only happened in the mornings. *Oh, Lordy...*

Mazie was snooping unashamedly when Fiona returned to the living room. She held out a small framed check for fifty dollars. "What's this?"

Fiona dropped her purse on a chair. "It's the first money I ever made as a professional artist. I was dead broke, and I needed so badly to cash it and pay my rent. But I decided to believe in my future and to believe there would be other checks coming. So far, I haven't had to break the glass."

Mazie nodded, returning the small frame to its spot on a bookshelf. "I know what you mean. Not the money part. My family has been fortunate in that way. But when I realized I didn't want to follow the boys into the family business, it was a struggle to decide what I was interested in—and then to make it happen. Now I sell jewelry in the historic district. I love my shop, and I do very well. It makes you proud, doesn't it? Women are always being underestimated. Drives me nuts."

Fiona grinned. Mazie was a firecracker. Fiona liked her. A lot. And although she had never had a real sister, Hartley's sibling was exactly the kind of female Fiona had envisioned when she wished for one.

Mazie handed over two twenties. "I don't know how much they'll cost at a convenience store. I've written down the brand I'd like to have. If you have to pick a second choice, I'll take what I can get."

"Then let's go."

Mazie insisted on driving. Her car was a current-year model that smelled of leather and a whiff of expensive perfume. Fiona settled into the passenger seat with a sigh of appreciation. Her own car was not a clunker, but as cute as it was, the little VW Bug was no match for high-end automotive luxury.

Mazie's driving was the real shock. She tended to talk with her hands, and though she didn't commit any traffic violations, her style was a little too kamikaze for Fiona's comfort.

They pulled up with a screech in front of a gas station mini-mart. Mazie gripped the wheel, her gaze anxious. "Hurry, please. I don't want to take any chances."

Inside the small shop, Fiona found the appropriate aisle quickly. Choices were limited, but the store did have the brand Mazie had requested. Instead of a duo, Fiona grabbed up four, then rounded the corner and plopped them down on the counter in sets of two. "I'll pay for these separately," she said, feeling the heat roll from her chest to her throat to her face.

It was ridiculous to be embarrassed, but this was her first pee-on-a-stick experience. The young store clerk didn't bat an eye. He rang up the two sales, dispensed change and Fiona's credit card slip, and went back to his phone.

Fiona had made a point of bringing a large leather tote instead of the smaller wristlet she often carried. Both women had valid reasons for keeping this little shopping excursion under the radar.

Fiona sauntered back outside as if she bought quads of pregnancy tests every day of the week. She opened the car door, slid into her seat and handed Mazie the white paper bag. "All set," she said breezily.

Mazie chewed her lip. "May I do this at your house?"

Weird. "Why?"

"I told you. I don't want to get J.B.'s hopes up. He hovers. And then it kills him when I'm sad."

"So how many times have you done this?"

"Not as many as you think. Twice maybe. Mostly it's just that my period starts, and then we know we have to wait another month. After this, I'll get out of your way, I swear."

"You're not in my way," Fiona muttered. Though she had to admit the entire scenario was freaking her out. What if Hartley showed up while Mazie was around?

Back at the house, Fiona showed Mazie the tiny guest bath in the hallway. Once Mazie was tucked away, Fiona darted into her studio bathroom and locked the door. Good sense dictated waiting until her guest had departed, but she couldn't.

Her fingers trembled as she opened the box and read the directions. This was a bad sit-com...right? The hero's sister in one bathroom. His lover in another. Both women possibly pregnant.

Fiona did what had to be done and waited. The message on the stick was swift and un-equivocal. Positive. *Pregnant.*

She stared at it blankly. One part of her brain acknowledged she was in shock. The other more emotional compartment wanted to scream it from the housetop. She was having Hartley's baby!

Later tonight there would be time for the second test. To double-check. It wasn't really necessary, was it? Her body had already com-municated the truth in rare form.

A sound from the other part of the house drew her back to the present. Though she was shaky and weak, she concentrated fiercely. *Wrap the evidence in tissues. Tuck it away. Stash the incriminating boxes in a back cor-ner of the cabinet.*

Then she washed her hands, splashed water on her face and went in search of Mazie.

Hartley's sister was still in the bathroom when Fiona passed by. But moments later, she came out and joined Fiona in the living room. Instead of being seated, she stood in the middle of the rug, her expression shell-shocked. "I did them both," she whispered. "They were positive."

Hartley had tried to give Fiona her space, really he had. But all day, missing her had been like a throbbing toothache. He still couldn't believe she had tossed him out of her bed.

He'd kept busy. The fixer-upper a few streets over from Fiona's charming bungalow would be his in less than two weeks—a cash sale. His own place out at the golf course already had several offers on the table. Hartley was leaving the minutiae up to the real estate agent. As long as he didn't lose money on the deal, he'd be satisfied.

The one detail he hadn't worked out was where he would live in the meantime. Even optimistically, it would take a couple of months to make his new three-story brick home moderately habitable.

Several of the potential buyers for the golf course house wanted to take possession ASAP. Hartley could go to a hotel, of course. For that matter, J.B. and Mazie would take him in. Still, they were relative newlyweds, even now. Besides, Hartley didn't want to make things awkward between Mazie and Jonathan.

Which left one obvious solution. Fiona.

He pulled up in front of her house and frowned. What was his sister doing here?

Indignation bubbled in his chest. Fiona wouldn't share secrets that weren't hers...would she? He thought he knew her that well, but then again, he hadn't bargained on being booted out of the stubborn woman's warm, comfy bed in the dead of night, so what did he know?

He banged on the door with his fist, unable to decide if he was suspicious or angry, or both. "Fiona! Let me in." When he reached for the knob, it turned easily. He opened the door and found two women staring at him, looking guilty as hell.

Both of them resembled kids with their hands

caught in the cookie jar. "What's going on?" he asked.

Mazie and Fiona blushed. His sister looked happy. Fiona's expression was less easily defined. She wasn't smiling at him, and she didn't seem particularly glad to see him.

Mazie broke the silence. "Nothing's going on, silly. I dropped by because I wanted to get to know your girlfriend."

"I'm not his girlfriend," Fiona said quickly. "We're friends. That's all."

Hartley's sister waved a hand. "Friend. Girlfriend. Who cares about labels these days?"

Fiona went on the offensive, her gaze cool. "The question is, Hartley, why are *you* here? It's hard to have closure when you keep turning up like a bad penny. You walked right into my house."

Mazie snickered, her hand over her mouth.

Hartley closed the door and leaned against it. "You were the one wanting closure, Fiona, not me. Do you really want to discuss this in front of my gossipy sister?"

"Hey," Mazie cried. "That's not nice."

Fiona aligned herself with the fairer sex.

"Mazie and I were sharing a moment. You're intruding."

Mazie flung herself at Hartley, wrapping her arms around his neck and threatening to strangle him. "No, he's not. I'm so *glad* you're home."

Her tight hug and the kiss on his cheek caught something in his chest and made his eyes damp. "I love you, too, sis," he said gruffly.

His eyes met Fiona's over Mazie's head. "What if I take the two of you to dinner? We can call J.B. and have him meet us at the restaurant. It'll be fun."

Inexplicably, his sister blushed again and looked at Fiona as if for help. "You're sweet to offer, Hartley, but I'll take a rain check. J.B. and I have plans tonight."

Hartley shrugged. "Fair enough. I'd still like to show you something before you leave. We can all three pile into my car. Won't take us long. Twenty minutes, tops."

"So mysterious," Fiona said.

He eluded his sister and curled an arm around Fiona's waist. Her hair smelled like raspberries. He loved raspberries. "I need your artistic expertise." He kissed her nose. She leaned into him. Progress...

Mazie glanced at her watch. "I'm in. But we need to hurry."

As the women climbed into his car, Fiona in the front, Mazie in the back, Hartley realized he was nervous. These two people were important in his life. Their opinions mattered.

When he pulled up in front of the huge dilapidated brick structure with the overgrown yard, he smiled inwardly. Attached to the small for-sale sign was another placard that said Sold. He'd done a lot in twenty-four hours. Moving ahead. Writing off the past.

Mazie leaned over the front seat. "What is this place, Hartley?"

Fiona stared through the windshield, her expression pensive.

He shrugged, gripping the steering wheel. "I bought it today. I'm going to fix it up and live here temporarily. Then sell it later for twice the price if I'm lucky."

"What do you know about renovating an old house?" His sister's concern was valid.

"Not much more than I've seen on TV," he

admitted. "But I can learn. I have no illusions about doing all the work myself."

Fiona chewed her lip. "It looks like a wreck. Have you even been inside?"

She nailed him on that one. Perhaps she had already come to recognize his impulsive nature. "I saw lots of pictures," he said. "And I bought it for a rock-bottom price. It's a good investment."

Mazie pinched his arm. "And it's in Fiona's neighborhood...right?"

Fee frowned. "But you have a house. On a golf course somewhere. You told me about it."

"I listed it this morning. Had two offers before lunch and more this afternoon. I'll likely make a handy profit."

Mazie nodded. "He never really liked that house anyway. It served a purpose at the time." She patted his shoulder. "I think it's wonderful, Hartley. I have several friends in the construction business. I'm sure I can round up some experts here and there."

He squeezed his sister's fingers briefly, but his gaze held Fiona's, daring her to look away. "I was hoping Fee would be willing to help me from an artistic perspective. So I can flip it successfully."

Fiona stared at him, her chest rising and falling rapidly as if she were out of breath. "Work is really busy for me right now."

He brushed the back of his hand across her soft cheek, gazing at her with determination and sexual intent. "In the evenings, then. I'll feed you, and I'll pay you for your time."

Mazie fell back in her seat, beaming. "Of course she'll help you. Right, Fiona?"

Fiona felt pressured by the sibling duo. These two thought they could throw money at a problem and everything would break their way. They hadn't a clue what it was like to be hungry or alone or to lack confidence.

Instead of answering directly, she put a hand on the door. "Can we peek in the windows?"

Hartley's face lightened, his enthusiasm contagious. "Of course. Once the paperwork is further along, I'll get the real estate agent to give us a tour."

"Is it even safe?" she asked.

"I suppose we'll find out."

The three of them walked up the path, dodg-

ing plants that tried to grab their hair and avoid-
ing broken glass where kids had tossed beer
bottles while trespassing. Mazie wrinkled her
nose. "How long has this place been empty?"

Fiona surveyed the three-story facade. "I pass
by this way now and again. I seem to remember
the owner dying a year or more ago. Maybe it's
taken this long for the heirs to decide to sell it."

"I can't imagine they would want to keep
it." Mazie frowned. "This place is kind of a
dump, Hartley. I was imagining a diamond in
the rough, not a total disaster."

He tried the front door, but of course it was
locked. "The house has good bones. I have faith
in her." He took Fiona's wrist and drew her
closer. "Peek in this window here. Tell me what
you see."

Even from the vantage point of a filthy pane
of glass, Fiona was charmed. The house looked
like a museum inside, a museum with chunks
of ceiling missing and peeling wallpaper, but
a museum nevertheless. The ornate cornices
and hardwood floors hearkened back to an earlier time. If the double winding staircase at the
back of the hallway was intact, Hartley might
indeed have found a hidden gem.

"It's got potential," she said grudgingly. What she wanted to say was *Why are you buying a house near me?* It didn't make sense. Hartley was a man without a country, a displaced person. He had come back to his old life, but the world had moved on without him. So he was inventing a spot for himself.

If the only reason he was here with her was because he had no place else to go, she wasn't interested. She'd had a lifetime of not belonging. Now, her small house and her burgeoning career were all hers.

It wasn't that she didn't have room in her life for Hartley. The truth was, if and when she finally fell in love and got married, she wanted a relationship where her husband thought she hung the moon.

Hartley liked having sex with her. She was a handy distraction from his family woes. But she deserved more than that. If she really was pregnant, she *wanted* this baby. More than anything. Yet Hartley had said unequivocally that he wasn't interested in being a father.

If she told him and he tried to *do the right thing*, she couldn't bear it. He'd left her twice.

Even if he tried to change his tune, how could she ever trust him or his motives?

Mazie squawked when she glanced at her watch. "Oh, heck. I've got to run. Take me back to my car, Hartley. I still have to go by the shop before I head home. J.B. will shoot me if I'm late."

"Since when is your husband a clock puncher?"

"We've both been working too much lately. We made a pact to have dinner together every night."

In the car on the way back, Fiona glanced over her shoulder. She and Mazie exchanged glances. Hartley's sister had shining eyes and a palpable air of excitement. This meal with J.B. tonight would be momentous.

As soon as Hartley pulled up at the curb, Mazie was out of the car and on her way. Hartley stared after her. "She sure was in a good mood."

Fiona nodded. "Of course she is. She has a husband who adores her. It's a gorgeous day. And her long-lost brother is finally home."

"I wasn't lost," Hartley muttered. "I simply chose to fly under the radar for a few months."

"Your silence hurt them," Fiona said. "If they

stumble onto the other secrets you're keeping, it will be even worse this time. Surely you see they need to know what you found out in Switzerland."

Hartley glared at her. "You're not going to give up on this, are you? So what about you, Fiona? Shouldn't you be digging up all your family secrets, sordid or otherwise?"

She gasped, stunned by the attack. "Excuse me," she said carefully. "I'm going in the house now."

He reached for her arm. "Stop. Wait. Dammit, I'm sorry, Fee. I have a temper. You're only trying to help. I get that."

She trembled, close to tears. This was a bad time to fall apart. "Let's get something straight, Hartley. If you're telling the truth when you say you want to be with me, then I need to believe it. So far in our relationship, I've been either a convenient booty call or a buffer for your messed-up family dynamics. Since I'm not interested in either of those roles, I suggest you get your life in order before you come here again."

Eight

Mazie opened the front door of the gorgeous row house that was now *hers*, as well as her husband's, and slipped inside. She wanted to shower and change before running into J.B. Tonight was special.

Upstairs in her decadent walk-in closet, she perused her choices. After their wedding, J.B. had taken one of the smaller bedrooms and converted it for his bride. Now she had a tiny sitting area and plenty of space for her wardrobe.

He spoiled her.

She loved it.

Even now, it was hard to believe she was actually *married* to the handsome hunk who had been her teenage crush. J.B. had been a bit of a rascal in his youth. He'd broken Mazie's heart badly on one particular, memorable occasion. After years of keeping a careful distance from each other here in Charleston, they had reconnected when her little jewelry shop ended up right in the middle of one of J.B.'s big real estate projects.

One thing led to another, and now she was happily married to a reformed bad boy. She smirked as she grabbed a quick shower and changed into black pants and a royal blue silk top. She and J.B. worked hard. This commitment to having dinner together every night had not always been easy, but it was an intimate time they had both come to cherish.

She was ridiculously nervous. Mostly because she hadn't decided whether or not to bring J.B. in on her secret yet. It was too early to get excited. She knew that. She needed an appointment with her ob-gyn before she got her hopes up. No point in telling him when she wasn't absolutely sure.

Over-the-counter pregnancy tests weren't completely reliable.

In the dining room, she found J.B. scrolling through email on his phone while he waited for her. Immediately, he put the phone aside and drew her in for a long, slow kiss. "How's my best girl?" he drawled when she was flushed and breathless. The man was an Olympic-level kisser. World class.

"I'm great," she said. *Maybe really great.*

J.B.'s fiftysomething housekeeper was a Southern-style cook who had learned to tilt her wonderful recipes toward healthier options without sacrificing taste. Mazie might have gained five pounds since the wedding, but it was worth every ounce.

The first course was Caesar salad with freshly made dressing and shaved Parmesan. "I came by the shop this afternoon between site visits," J.B. said, "but you were gone."

"I went to see Hartley's girlfriend."

One masculine eyebrow lifted. "Mazie. I warned you about matchmaking. Hartley's a big boy. He can make his own decisions."

She stabbed a piece of lettuce. "He hasn't done so well this past year," she muttered. "I can't stand to see the way he and Jonathan are with each other. It's *wrong*," she said, her eyes unexpectedly filling with tears. "They're brothers. Twins, for God's sake. Best friends."

J.B. reached across the table and took her hand. "They'll work through it eventually. Hartley's home now. That's a start."

"Can't you talk to them? Either? Both? Jonathan is being all *scowly* and buttoned-up and Hartley is...well, I don't know. He's acting weird. Did you know he bought a house today?"

J.B. blinked. "He has a house."

"Not anymore. He listed it this morning. Already has offers."

"So where is this *new* house?"

"Three blocks away from Fiona."

"Ah. The plot thickens."

"I dropped by to talk to her late this afternoon, and Hartley showed up, insisting that we look at his new toy. It's a huge run-down place. Going to need tons of work."

"Sounds expensive."

She sat back and frowned. "Are you taking any of this seriously?"

J.B. grinned. "I take *you* seriously. They're grown men, sweetheart. Give them time."

"Did Jonathan ever tell you why Hartley left?

Or what made Jonathan so angry he will hardly speak Hartley's name?"

"He didn't, my love. Whatever this is feels like a betrayal so deep Jonathan can't get past it."

Mazie chewed her lip. It didn't take a psychologist to see that she was dwelling on this Hartley/Jonathan rift to put off telling J.B. what she suspected was true. It was so scary.

"Fiona knows."

Jonathan frowned. "Are you positive?"

"I asked her. She told me. Not the details," Mazie said quickly. "But that Hartley very recently confided in her."

"So she's important to him."

"Looks that way. But I don't think he knows it yet."

The housekeeper came in with the main course, and the topic was shelved for the moment. By the time dessert rolled around, Mazie had come to a decision. If she was going to wait for confirmation until she could see her doctor, then she wanted J.B. waiting with her.

While he drank his coffee, she watched him. He'd been almost a part of their family since they were all kids. It was impossible to imagine her life without him. He was funny and irreverent and never met a stranger. He would make a wonderful father.

Her stomach flopped and twisted. "J.B.?" she said.

His gaze met hers over the rim of his cup. "Hmm?"

"What if we go upstairs early tonight?"

A dark streak of red bloomed on his chiseled cheekbones. His eyes glittered with strong emotion. "Is that what you want?"

Their sex life had suffered in recent months. It was impossible to make love anymore without thinking about whether or not the baby they so desperately wanted was being conceived. And then every month when Mazie got her period, they both mourned.

"It is," she said.

He lurched to his feet, bumping the table. "I'll tell Mrs. P. to finish up tomorrow. That my dear wife wants my body."

Mazie covered her mouth, laughing. "You wouldn't dare."

"Watch me."

In truth, Mazie had no idea what he said to the housekeeper, but in less than half an hour, the kitchen was pristine and the older woman was gone.

Mazie wandered the living room aimlessly, praying for courage. J.B. found her there.

He paused in the doorway like a gunslinger walking into a saloon. "Alone at last," he said, the words gruff.

She went to him and sighed when he immediately folded her close in his arms. There was no place she would rather be. Not ever.

"I need to tell you something before we go upstairs," she said.

He kissed the top of her head. "I'm listening."

She pulled back, searching his face. Wanting to judge his reaction. "I think I'm pregnant."

His big frame went rigid. "Are you positive?"

"Not a hundred percent. I did a couple of store-bought tests. But I'll need to see my doctor. I can't get an appointment until Tuesday."

He cupped her face in his hands. His eyes were damp. "God, I want this to be true. So damn much. I love you, Mazie."

She swallowed hard. "I'm scared."

His frown was swift. "About what?"

"Lisette has suffered two miscarriages already." Tears she couldn't stem spilled from her eyes. "What if that happens to me?"

"It won't," he said firmly. "We've had trouble *getting* pregnant. There's no reason you should worry about *losing* a baby."

She snuggled into his embrace a second time, drawing strength from the sheer physicality of his body. "I don't *feel* pregnant," she whispered. "Shouldn't I feel something? Shouldn't I know?"

J.B. stroked her hair. "You're gonna have to relax, Mazie."

"I know. I think it would help my stress level if you would play intermediary between Jonathan and Hartley."

"So that's how it's going to be, brat." He took her hand and headed for the stairs. "I get it."

"What?" she cried innocently.

He stopped halfway up to the second floor, his smile lopsided. "You think I'm going to say yes to you for an entire nine months."

"Is that a problem?" She gave him a smug grin, unbuttoning her shirt slowly.

His hot gaze started at her eyes and drifted lower, locking on the curves of her breasts, telegraphing his intent. "Not at all. Because I'm going to keep you on bed rest with me."

She giggled, shoving him in front of her. "That's not even a thing, J.B. Vaughan."

On the landing, he scooped her into his arms and carried her the rest of the way. "Whatever it takes, my love. Whatever it takes."

Fiona nearly called Mazie for advice, a woman she barely knew. That's how freaked out she was. After Mazie dashed away earlier, headed home to rendezvous with her husband, Fiona had made awkward excuses to Hartley and locked herself inside the cottage.

She couldn't face him right now. For all her big words about how wrong it was to keep secrets from his family, Fiona was doing the same thing. Keeping a huge plot twist from the man who might possibly be a father very soon.

That evening, she puttered around the house, dusting…tidying up. Since it was far too early for nesting, the only logical explanation was that she was losing her marbles. Popping her cork. Her well-oiled life was off the tracks.

How could she tell him she might be pregnant? Wouldn't it be smarter to find out for sure first?

And then what? He'd spoken his piece un-equivocally. *I won't have children. I choose not to take that chance.*

Remembering his words hurt. Badly. It was as if he was repudiating everything that was happening to her. Of course he didn't know. How could he? That didn't make her anxiety and incredulity any less real and painful.

She managed to keep Hartley at bay over the weekend...barely. He called. He texted. He asked to come by and see her.

Her work was her excuse. She needed blocks of uninterrupted time. He claimed to under-stand. But each time they spoke, she felt his frustration increase. Worst of all, she missed him. A lot.

Having him in her bed each night would have been a wonderful comfort. Even feeling the way she did, she wanted him. As it was, she slept alone and awoke every morning barely in time to dash to the bathroom.

Her reflection in the mirror was appalling. Her hair was lank and dull. She had lost weight. Cooking was too much trouble. All she could tolerate, even later in the day, was chicken broth and dry crackers. When her stash ran dry, she used a grocery service.

Amid the stretches of feeling sorry for herself—and when she could stand for chunks of time—she worked on her paintings. Only then did she feel anything at all like normal. The repetitive brushstrokes calmed her. The colors that spread forth on the canvas filled the yawning chasm in her chest with purpose and joy.

In her heart, she knew she was pregnant. The doctor's appointment she had wrangled at the last minute for Wednesday morning was only going to confirm her status as a mother-to-be. So what was she going to do about it?

She wanted the baby. Desperately. There was no doubt about that. Thinking about holding her own tiny infant in her arms made her heart sing. But uncertainty about Hartley's reaction tempered her excitement. Could she be a single mom?

Sunday night, she forced herself to take a shower and wash her hair. The nausea had finally subsided some. But her energy level was nil.

At eight, she put on soft cotton pajamas and

curled up to watch a movie. Hartley's text came through before the first credit rolled.

Do you mind if I stop by for a few?

Ah, damn. The way her heart leaped in her chest told her the truth. She couldn't put him off any longer...didn't want to, for that matter.

I'm home. What time will you get here?

I'm in my car out at the street.

His comical emoji actually made her laugh.

Come on in.

She unlocked the door and watched him walk up the path. Everything inside her warmed and settled. Hartley made her world a little better. A lot happier. She could argue with herself all she wanted, but it was true. He was the one she had been waiting for...her knight in shining armor.

Could a black sheep prodigal make the leap to hero?

She gripped the edge of the door, white-knuckled. "Hello."

He paused to kiss her gently. "Hello, yourself. You must have been working hard. Is the project coming along?"

"It is," she said. That wasn't entirely a lie.

"These are for you." He'd brought more roses, blush pink this time. Without asking, he headed for the kitchen and dug out the vase. She followed, standing in the doorway to watch him. Were all women so emotional about the men who made them pregnant?

When he was satisfied with the arrangement, he dried his hands and set the vase on the table. "You look tired. I won't stay long." His smile was sweet, catching her off guard. "I missed you these last few days," he said.

She swallowed. "I missed you, too. Come sit with me in the living room," she said. "I want to tell you something."

Not the whole truth and nothing but the truth. That conversation would have to wait for a few more days. After the official doctor's appointment.

They perched on the sofa together. Hartley wrapped an arm around her shoulders as if it were the most natural thing in the world. Though arousal flooded her veins, it was more like a slow, warm river than licks of fire. Hartley was back in Charleston to stay. They had time. For now.

"How's the new purchase?" she asked.

He yawned and leaned his head against the back of the sofa. "I may have bitten off more than I can chew. Although, I'm discovering that punishing physical labor does wonders for clearing a man's brain. I've been working in the yard since I don't have the keys yet."

"Have you tried to talk to your brother?"

She felt him stiffen slightly. "I ran into him a few nights ago. It didn't go well."

"I'm sorry." The faint bitterness in his voice told her he was wounded by the rift with his twin.

Hartley rubbed the top of her shoulder with his thumb. "What did you want to tell me?"

"I know you disagree with me about whether or not you should tell your siblings about Switzerland. But I have some experience with secrets. It concerns my parents."

He pulled away from her and groaned. "Please don't make me feel worse. I never should have

lost my temper. Your past is none of my business."

Her smile was wistful. "You've told me your
sordid secrets. I think it's time for you to hear
mine."

Nine

Sordid secrets. Hell. Now she was quoting his unforgivable words back to him. He felt like whatever was lower than pond scum.

Fiona stood up and wrapped her arms around her waist. Her pj's were not terribly thin, but he could see she wasn't wearing a bra. He was swamped by a wave of tenderness mixed with lust. It was an unfamiliar combo, and he didn't know what to do with the feelings.

"Please don't," he begged. "God knows, you don't owe me any explanations."

She stared at him, big gray-blue eyes filled with feminine emotions he couldn't decipher. "I spent my whole life wondering who I was.

I lived in an actual orphanage…a children's home, until I was eight. After that, they had to move some of us out to make room for more. I was labeled *amenable*, so I went into foster care. It wasn't terrible. Some of the families were pretty wonderful. But it was all temporary. I knew it and everyone else did, too. The odds of getting adopted at that age are like winning the lottery."

She'd barely started and already her story was tearing him apart, leaving him raw inside. While he'd been living in a veritable castle, Fiona had been tossed around by governmental red tape.

"I don't need to hear this," he said. *I don't want to hear it.*

Fiona was on a mission. "When I was seventeen and a half, they told me I could begin the process of applying for my records to be opened. Then, when I reached my eighteenth birthday, I would have the option of knowing or not knowing. My choice."

"And what did you do?"

"I filled out the paperwork, and I started dreaming dreams. Now that I was going to be an adult, I was sure my biological parents would want to know me. I wasn't on drugs. I had graduated near the top of my high school class. I was not going to *ask* them for anything at all. The only thing I wanted was to be able to look them in the eye and see where I came from. To understand why I was allergic to apricots. To know if it was my dad or my mother who gave me my artistic ability, or maybe a grandparent. To finally study my family tree."

"Ah, hell, darlin'—" This story didn't have a happy ending. He knew it before she even told him the rest.

Fiona ran her hands through her hair, her eyes scrunched shut as if she didn't want to remember. "When my birthday rolled around, everything was an open book. The details were sparse, but they were there. I came from a small rural county up the coast. Rampant poverty. Poor schools. High numbers of opioid deaths. My birth mother was fifteen when she had me. She hemorrhaged after the delivery and died before they could save her."

"Good God." The long-ago tragedy was stunning. "And your father?"

"He was in jail for drug possession the night I was born. The following day he was released, but on the way to the hospital, he crashed his car into a tree."

"Because he was high?"

"Yes."

"Surely you had grandparents."

"The official report listed four names. I followed up on each one. All deceased. At that point, I no longer had any interest in looking for cousins or aunts and uncles. I was done."

He went to her and held her, feeling the fine tremors that racked her slender body. "I'm sorry," he said.

Fiona rested her cheek against his chest. "It was wretched," she said. "I felt so foolish for all those silly dreams I had spun in my imagination."

"Dreams are not bad things."

"No. But despite everything I learned, I didn't regret seeking out the answers. I decided I wouldn't be defined by my origin story. There was more to me than that. I set goals, and I pursued my passions, and I made peace with my past. Knowing is *always* better than not knowing, Hartley. That's why you need to tell Jonathan and Mazie about their mother."

He hadn't expected her to turn this on him,

but he should have seen it coming. "There's a difference," he said stubbornly, releasing her and going to stare out the window.

"How?"

He shot her a look over his shoulder. "Jonathan and Mazie don't have any 'blanks' like you did. They know who they are. They're *not* wondering and wishing. So they aren't struggling to find answers."

"But the truth they believe is a lie."

He ground his teeth. There was merit in what she was saying. Still, other factors made him leery of sharing the information with his siblings. "Our father just died. I think that's enough trauma for one season. Maybe you and I can agree to disagree on this point."

"I'm pretty stubborn about things that are important to me."

He found a smile, wanting to shift the mood to less volatile topics. "Duly noted." Pulling out his phone, he flipped to the photo icon. "I actually came tonight to ask about you doing a job for me. A commission."

"I've got a couple of big things in the works, Hartley."

"This will be small. Mazie's birthday is coming up in a few weeks, and I wanted to surprise her." He showed her a photo. "This is Mazie and J.B. at their wedding reception. See how he's looking at her. I know she would love to have you paint this for them."

"That's not really what I do. I focus on outdoor subjects. Landscapes. Birds. That kind of thing."

"But you *could* do it…right? Mazie would flip. She's been singing your praises to me. She thinks you're phenomenally talented, and I agree."

"Flattery will get you everywhere," Fiona said. Her laughter loosened the knot in his chest that had appeared when she told him about her parents. "Text me the photo. I'll fool around with a sketch and see what I can do."

"Thank you." He pulled up her number, sent the photo and set his phone on the coffee table. "How about a kiss before I go?"

Fiona didn't want him to go. Not at all. She wanted to burrow into his embrace and feel his hands on her body and forget for a few moments that she was in big trouble.

She cocked her head and stared at him. His

innocent expression had to be at least 75 percent fake. He knew what his kisses did to a woman. "Are you asking permission?"

Hartley tugged her toward the sofa again and sat down, tumbling her onto his lap. "I want you, Fee. To a degree that's damn scary. What do you say to that?" Brown eyes stared into hers. The humor was gone now. In its place was pure male hunger. Or maybe not so pure. His expression promised all sorts of mischief. All sorts of pleasure.

Her body responded instantly, softening, yearning. She couldn't even barter for a short-lived fling, because she was growing a baby. A baby who was his. How was she going to tell him? For all her big speeches about the danger of secrets, she was scared spitless to expose hers.

"I want you, too," she said, no longer able to pretend that she didn't. There was no reason to dissemble. Soon enough he would find out that her body was fully prepared to welcome his. Damp heat at her core yearned for his rigid length to fill her and drive her mad.

That's what it was. Madness. She should tell him he didn't need a condom. Explain what happened on that night three months ago. Ask what they were going to do about it.

All the reasons not to make love to him tonight were valid, but she shoved them aside in the pursuit of happiness. Carpe diem. Worry about tomorrow another day.

He twisted one of her curls around his finger. "I care about you, Fiona. This isn't casual for me."

His sober promise should have made her heart sing. At any other moment in her life, that declaration would have been exciting and perfect. As it was, her anxiety ratcheted higher.

"There's nothing wrong with casual. We're both young and unattached. I'm not expecting any commitment at this point."

Her words seemed to bother him. He frowned. "Have you been with a lot of men, Fee? For some reason, I got the impression you were a bit more fastidious about your sexual partners. Am I wrong?"

Now she was caught in the crosshairs. If she said yes, he might ultimately wonder if the baby was his. But a negative response—an admission that he'd been her only sexual partner in the last three years—might reveal more than she was willing for him to know.

She reached up to stroke his masculine jaw-line. The shadow of a late-day beard gave him a rakish air. "What we stumbled into at the wedding last year and then again three months ago was definitely special. We have chemistry. I'm not denying that. But I have a life and a career that don't really intersect well with yours. Our goals are different." *I have a baby on the way, and I'm thrilled about creating a family.*

"Meaning what?"

"You and I are friends. Temporary lovers. I like plain speaking. I don't need flowery compliments or promises about the future."

"Is this because I'm homeless and unemployed?" His wry grin was boyish and charming and totally unfair.

She rolled her eyes. "You're a wealthy man. I can ignore your money as long as we're playing at this relationship."

"Hell, Fiona. I've never had this level of negotiation before sex. Then again, sex with you is worth a little extra trouble. So what you're saying is that your art and your career are more important than flesh and blood relationships?"

"Of course not. Don't twist my words."

"Then *you* explain it."

How could she? All Fiona wanted was a family and a home of her own. Hartley, on the other hand, was going to be furious when he found out about the baby. If he wanted the unvarnished truth, he could have it. "We had great sex, but that's all it was."

His face darkened with displeasure. "If a man had said that, he'd be pilloried. What are you so afraid of, Fiona? I won't ask for anything you aren't willing to give. We're good together. Admit it."

"I've already admitted it, Hartley."

"If we sleep together right now, are you going to let me spend the night?" His pointed question caught her off guard. Guilt turned her stomach queasy and her face red. He couldn't be here when morning came. Not the way things were with her right now.

She lifted her chin, meeting his gaze calmly. "No. I like my privacy and my personal space. There's nothing wrong with that."

"Okay then." Before she could do more than gasp and flail in his arms, he flipped her onto her back and started unbuttoning her pajama top. She was paralyzed by her need for him. When she was bare from the waist up, he paused and sucked in a breath. "You are so damned beautiful."

He stroked one nipple with a fingertip. His touch made her skin burn. "Hartley…"

"What?" He sprawled beside her, partly reclining beside the low sofa. When he leaned over her, took that same nipple in his teeth and tugged gently, she groaned.

"Don't stop," she whispered. Heat rolled through her body, making her shift restlessly. Had she closed the curtains? Rational thought fled when he dragged her pajama bottoms down her legs along with her plain cotton undies. Now she lay there completely naked, like a not-so-virgin sacrifice.

The look on his face threatened to incinerate her. His words were ragged. "Each time I leave you I think I might have exaggerated this in my mind. And then we're together again, and I know it's all true. My hands are shaking, and I can barely breathe. That's not normal for a guy my age. I don't know what happens when I touch you…when we touch each other."

The trace of bewilderment in the midst of his

arousal reflected her own conflicted emotions. Only now, she had the added bonus of worrying about whether she had a baby bump that would tip him off.

"Enough talking," she muttered.

He chuckled, but stood and ripped off his clothes. His sex was stiff and eager. Had he always been so...*big*? Maybe it was because the lights were on or because he loomed over her.

"Let's go the the bedroom," she pleaded.

A dark flush rode high on his cheeks. The skin stretched taut over the planes of his face. He was the conquering hero...the ravaging marauder. The intensity of his focus on *her* made her shiver.

"No," he said bluntly. "Can't wait."

He moved her like a rag doll, sitting down on the sofa and spreading her legs across his body. Before she could do more than gasp, he entered her with a forceful push. His back arched. He cursed softly. And then he captured her mouth in a frantic, hungry kiss.

This position made her feel deliciously vulnerable. Her hormones went wild, plunging her into a quick, sharp climax that didn't last nearly long enough. "More," she demanded.

"Whatever the lady wants."

Seconds later he tumbled them both to the floor. Her simple rug might never look the same to her again. He lifted one of her ankles onto his shoulder and thrust hard, all the way to her womb. The pleasure was a sharp-edged jolt, so searing, she wondered for a moment if they should be doing this. What did she know about being pregnant?

It was all theoretical until it happened to you.

Then he bit the inside of her thigh and she forgot to worry about anything but the magic they were creating together.

Hartley braced himself on his arms, slowing his movements until both of them were panting.

"Did you lose your way?" she asked, the words undeniably petulant.

Her pique made his masculine grin broaden. "It's called building the tension."

"Did you read this in some manual?"

"Are you criticizing my technique?"

She reached up and brushed the lock of hair from his damp forehead. It fell immediately back over his eyebrow. "This isn't casual for me either," she whispered, admitting defeat.

Her words stunned him visibly. She saw the shift in his gaze. The flare of heat. The exultation.

Gently, he disengaged their bodies and picked her up in his arms, a feat which took considerable strength considering she was on the floor.

"I wasn't done," she complained.

"Patience, Fee." In her narrow hallway, he bumped the bedroom door open with his hip and carried her to the bed. "I need soft sheets for the finale."

"Since when?"

He kissed her nose. "Since I decided to impress you with my romantic prowess."

It wasn't even funny, because it was true. Somehow he had managed to inject tenderness into their sexual insanity. That scared her so very badly. Because he was not going to be able to give her what she wanted and needed. He'd already told her that.

Sex, he could do. Family and forever, not so much.

She'd never had much luck with forevers. Even worse, this particular situation was snake-bit from the beginning.

"Come here," she said, holding out her arms.

He settled on top of her with a groan, resting his forehead against hers. There wasn't room between them for a sheet of paper, much less a secret of the enormity of hers.

What was she going to do?

"You're amazing, Fee," he said, filling her again, igniting the flame that had been banked for a time. "Wrap your legs around my waist."

When she did, he slid his hands under her ass and lifted her into his thrusts, giving both of them that extra measure of perfection they craved. She was close, so close.

Hartley shuddered and found his release, his breath warm on her cheek. His scent surrounded her, marking her sheets, making it impossible to pretend he didn't belong here. He was everywhere, filling her feminine bedroom with the force of his personality.

Rolling to one side, he stroked her sex, drawing a quick ragged sigh from her parched throat...sending her over the edge into warm, drowsy completion. "I love how you do that," she said.

"Do what?" he asked, the words slurred as his eyes drifted shut.

"You know exactly how to touch me."

He yawned, turning her and spooning her from behind. "It's my superpower, Fee."

Ten

Fiona woke up some time before dawn. Three things became clear in an instant. A very large, warm man had her wrapped in the pure bliss of his muscular arms. She had to pee. And her stomach had begun its morning calisthenics.

Her choices were limited. She could wake him up and physically shove him out of her house. That seemed mean and cold. She knew he hadn't meant to stay in defiance of her wishes. The two of them had been exhausted, Fiona from being pregnant, and Hartley from working at his new property.

So, if she wasn't willing to kick him out, she had to somehow make it to the bathroom and conceal the fact that morning sickness was about to take its toll. Again.

It was still dark, though the clock on her bedside table told her dawn wasn't far off. Slowly, she began easing out of Hartley's embrace. Even those small movements made her forehead break out in a cold sweat. The timing didn't make sense. Most people were sick during the first twelve weeks and finally got better in the second trimester...or so she had heard.

Then again, she'd known women who struggled with nausea the entire nine months, so who knew? Surely that wouldn't happen to her. She had to work. No work meant no pay. She certainly didn't want to get a reputation for being late on commissioned pieces. That wasn't who she was at all.

How was Hartley going to react? She wanted him to be happy, but that wasn't going to happen. Would he stay away from the child entirely? Or would he want even a minor role?

She had to tell him soon, so they could make plans for the future. Or so *she* could.

How could she keep from breaking her heart again and again if she and Hartley were always connected by this unexpected baby?

Thankfully, Hartley never stirred as she extracted herself from her predicament. Because her house was old, the bathroom was in the hall, not attached to her bedroom. She was able to throw up—twice—wash her face and tiptoe to the kitchen without disturbing her guest.

She didn't turn on the lights. Instead, she heated a mug of water in the microwave, added a tea bag and sat at the table, cradling the cup in her hands. Though it wasn't cold in the house, her shivers came from the inside out. Getting sick so violently left her feeling weak and shaky.

How did women stand this?

Gradually, she sipped her drink and her mood stabilized. Females had been handling this situation since the dawn of time. Fiona, herself, was more resilient that most. She'd had to be. This pregnancy was a curve she hadn't seen coming, but she would deal with it. Somehow.

Hartley startled her when he appeared in the doorway. There was enough light filtering through the window now for her to see that he had pulled on his pants and nothing else. Broad naked chest. Big bare man feet. He was an alien presence in her neatly feminine environment.

He raked a hand through his disheveled hair. "Sorry, Fee. I didn't stay on purpose." His voice was gruff and low, roughened by sleep.

She shrugged. "I know. We were both beat."

"I'll let myself out in a minute. I wanted to say goodbye."

Suddenly, she was teary and emotional. Stupid pregnancy hormones. She patted the table. "Come sit. Make coffee if you want to. Everything is there on the counter."

He glanced at the empty coffeepot. "What are you drinking?"

"Hot tea."

He put a hand on her shoulder and kissed the top of her head. "You doing okay, darlin'?"

His concern made her want to sob. She had to get a grip. "I've been pushing myself too hard lately. Not eating well. Feeling a little rotten today."

Once the coffeepot was burbling, he sat down beside her, rubbing her back. "Poor baby. What can I do to make it better?"

Rewrite the past. Tell me you'd love to have a dozen kids. Go away and never come back.

That last one was a huge, wretched lie. She wanted Hartley, and she wanted Hartley's child growing inside her. The kicker was, she didn't see a way for all of that to happen at the same time. Or ever.

"I'll be fine." She finished her tea, wishing she had a second cup.

"Why don't you take a day off?" he said. "You're the boss...right?"

"Yes. But being self-employed isn't for sissies. I have to think about things like quarterly taxes and health insurance premiums and mortgage payments."

"Ah." He stood and poured his coffee.

Fiona had been afraid the aroma might provoke her nausea, but thankfully, the smell was more comforting than anything else.

When Hartley sat down again, he studied her face. "I have a proposition for you," he said.

"It's too early in the morning for propositions."

He stroked the back of her hand with his thumb, sending tingles all over her body. "I've noticed a few things on the outside of your house...maintenance issues."

She interrupted him, feeling defensive about her beloved bungalow. "I know. I have a gutter that needs repairing. The roof lost a few shingles in that last storm. And the eaves need painting. It's a question of time and money, Hartley. I'll get to it." *Somehow.*

"Hear me out," he said. "I was thinking you might take in a boarder."

"A boarder? I only have one bedroom."

"True. But you have a very nice sofa. My new place is three streets away. It would be damned convenient for me to be close during the renovation. I could pay you rent, *and*," he said, "in the evenings, I could do a few handyman projects around your house."

Fiona closed her eyes. It was too early in the morning to be doing battle with a charmer. "I've already told you. I like my privacy and my space."

"Your studio is in the back of the house. I'll stay out of your way. You won't even know I'm here."

Her brain was muzzy. She could smell the scent of his sleep-warmed skin. All she wanted to do was go back to bed. *You won't even know I'm here.* Was he kidding? He filled up a room with his smile, which was exactly what got her into this mess in the first place.

From the moment she met the handsome groomsman who was going to walk her down the aisle at their mutual friends' wedding, she'd been a goner. Never had she met someone like Hartley. He was a combo of Viking marauder and Saint Bernard puppy. A stubborn alpha male who shaped the world to his liking but could laugh at himself and coax a woman into his bed with the twinkle in his eye. It was almost impossible for her to get mad at him, because he was so genuinely well-intentioned.

Hartley thought he could control the world, or at least his corner of it. That was why he was now estranged from his brother and why Fiona questioned telling him about the baby. He'd made up his mind not to have kids.

How would he react when she told him it was far too late?

She rubbed her temples. "You have plenty of money, Hartley. Find a hotel nearby. There are dozens of them."

"I lived on the road for over a year. I missed you, Fee. I missed having sex with you. I want to be here. Under your roof. Platonically if necessary until you can trust me again."

"Do you really think I'll sleep in my bed, and you'll be on the sofa? Come on, Hartley. I'm not that naive."

His thumb strayed up her arm, teasing the inside crook of her elbow. "That would be entirely up to you."

She pressed her thighs together. Now that her nausea had abated, arousal settled heavy in her abdomen. "I can't deal with this right now. Take me back to bed. It's too early. My brain doesn't work."

"Whatever you want, Fiona." He picked up her hand and sucked her pinky finger, his teeth raking her knuckle.

Holy hell. Had she always had that erogenous zone, or was pregnancy making her insatiable?

She jerked her hand away with a gasp she tried to turn into a cough. He had far too much ego as it was. No need for him to know he could reduce her to mush so easily. She fled down the hall. It wasn't even seven yet.

When she climbed under the covers, Hartley was right behind her. He nuzzled the back of her neck. "Do you want to sleep or screw?"

Her helpless giggle was mortifyingly girlish. "Do I have a choice?"

He leaned over her on one elbow, his expression dead sober. "You always have a choice, Fee."

"I'm sorry," she said quickly, feeling small. "I know that. I wasn't accusing you of anything. Well, except for being far too hard to resist."

A smile cracked his stoic expression. "A compliment? Wow, Fee, I don't know what to say."

She curled a hand behind his neck and pulled him down for a kiss. "You could say you'll give me a few days to think about this living together thing." *Maybe the morning sickness would subside soon, and Hartley's presence in her house wouldn't be such an issue.*

His tongue mated with hers, stealing her breath. "Fair enough."

Hartley didn't want to leave this woman or this bed at all. But he knew when to back off. If he couldn't win her over with cogent arguments, then he had to play to his strengths.

Though he couldn't take credit for whatever animal attraction had bewitched them, he'd be happy to use it to advance his cause.

It had alarmed him to wake up this morning and realize he was in bed alone. Fiona had seemed *twitchy* or something when he'd found her in the kitchen. As if he were indeed intruding on her personal space. Gradually, though, she had relaxed.

Now she was warm and affectionate and very clearly inclined to get the day off to a good start. He sifted his fingers through her rumpled curls. "Have I told you how much I love your hair?"

She grimaced. "I hated it for most of my life. I wasn't allowed to go the movies very often, but one of my foster moms had a huge DVD collection. I adored watching Gwyneth Paltrow in *Emma*. Kate Hudson in *How to Lose a Guy in 10 Days*. I envied their blond beauty, because I was the antithesis of that. Skinny and freckled and bashful."

"Neither of them can hold a candle to the woman you are now." He could see that little girl in his mind's eye. She had grown into a stunning human being. "You have a fire in you—maybe it's the creativity, I don't know. The moment we met each other at that damned wedding, I could no more have walked away from you than cut off my own arm. I wanted you desperately. Beyond all reason. Why do you think that is?"

She toyed with the shell of his ear. "Is that a serious question?"

Her touch sent little tingles of fire down his spine to his sex. "I think it is. I've always been suspicious of things I don't understand."

"But…?"

He slid his hand inside her pajama bottoms and found her center. She was warm and wet. He shook with the need to take and take and take until he blacked out from the pleasure. "But I'm learning to live with not knowing."

"Wow. What a sacrifice."

"Has anyone ever told you you've got a mean streak?"

"Most people think I'm adorable." She turned up her nose at him, clearly inclined to make fun of herself.

He chuckled. "Can't argue with that."

Sex with Fiona was never what he expected. In the midst of aching arousal, he still wanted to play endlessly. Her body was soft and supple. Small and yet powerfully feminine, strong enough to make him weak.

He hadn't entirely grown accustomed to the power she wielded. And he was pretty damned sure she had no idea the power was even there. Perhaps for now it was best she didn't. *Because he didn't know what he was going to do about the situation.*

Before climbing into bed, he had shucked his pants and boxers. Fiona wrapped her hand around his erection. His vision blurred. He was breathing like he had run a mile, and they had barely started.

He held his hand over hers. "Easy now. Let me unwrap you first."

"I'll help," she said. "You're being kind of slow."

His laugh was little more than a wheeze.

Between them they ripped off her pjs and clutched each other, naked skin to naked skin. It was enough to make him forget his name and every last one of his troubles.

His world narrowed to this bed. This woman.

Crap. Condoms. Did he have any left? He reached for the floor and his mangled clothing and found one more. Thank God.

His hands shook as he rolled it over his erection. "Foreplay?" he croaked.

She grabbed handfuls of his hair. "Not a chance. Get over here."

He filled her with one wild thrust. It was heaven and hell and every level of torment in between. Burying his face in her neck, he tried to count her heartbeats, to memorize the taste of her skin right below her ear.

Her body welcomed him, drew him in, held him captive. He had never been more glad to be a man. Whatever his sins—and there were many—he must have done something right. "I can't stop wanting you," he groaned.

Fiona sucked his bottom lip, sinking her teeth in just enough to sting. "Works both ways. But we can't stay in bed all day," she said, panting. "We're mature adults. We have to set boundaries."

He braced his weight on his hands for a minute and studied her face. Her cheeks were flushed, her throat abraded by the stubble on his chin. The red hair that was silky and soft fluffed out around her heart-shaped face. Before today, he hadn't noticed how that sweet pointed chin could be so stubborn.

"I never met a boundary I didn't want to smash."

Her eyes widened. The flush deepened. "I always thought of myself as a good girl."

"Just think of me as your black sheep lover. Ready to do any naughty thing your heart desires."

She squeezed his sex with her inner muscles, drawing a ragged groan from his dry throat.

"Make love to me, Hartley," she said. "Now."

It was a demand he was happy to oblige.

The feelings racketing around in his chest were foreign to him, dangerously so. He shoved them away, choosing to concentrate on the physical. When he knew Fiona was at the edge, he reached between their linked bodies and stroked her intimately.

She arched against him and climaxed, whispering his name over and over, making him feel like a king. Seconds later, he lost the fight with his own galloping need and came so hard he actually saw yellow spots dancing behind his closed eyelids.

Without meaning to, he slept again. But when he awoke fifteen minutes later, this time he wasn't alone.

He watched Fiona breathe, her breasts rising and falling almost imperceptibly. Gently, he

BOMBSHELL FOR THE BLACK SHEEP

twisted a curl around his finger, a game that was rapidly becoming one of his favorites.

The springy red-gold strands clung to his skin, alive with the passion he felt in her. In one blinding instant of clarity he understood that he couldn't be the man to break her heart. Not with the disappointments and challenges she had faced in her young life so far.

Fiona was a fighter, yes. Fiercely independent. Generous and brave. The right man could spend a lifetime making her happy...making up for all she had lost.

The big-ass problem was, Hartley didn't know if he was good enough or smart enough or deserving enough to be that guy. He'd been plowing ahead with his laundry list of wants and needs, determined to find his way into her life. But what or who did Fiona need?

When he stroked her cheek with the tip of his finger, her eyelashes fluttered open. Her gaze was dreamy. "Wow."

He couldn't stop his smug grin. "Ditto."

She stretched, causing all sorts of interesting reactions beneath the sheet. "I have to *work*, Hartley. Really, I do."

He rolled to a seated position and held up both hands. "I know, I know. I'm gone. But before I leave, one more thing."

Her hand settled on his thigh, perilously close to his semi-erect sex. "You never give up, do you?"

The temptation was almost overwhelming. Instead of giving in, he tried to be the better man. Lurching to his feet, he dressed clumsily, conscious of her gaze on his naked body. "No, no," he said. "I want to take you out on a date Friday night. It's a charity gala, black-tie. My father is receiving a posthumous award. Apparently, despite everything, my family wants me to be there."

Fiona raised up on her elbows. "Well, of course they do. That's lovely, Hartley."

"I want you to come with me, Fiona. Dinner, dancing. The formalities will be brief."

"I'd love to," she said simply.

"Really?" His disappointment at having to leave her bed was appeased. "I thought we might stay overnight at a small hotel near the event site. So we can indulge in champagne and stroll through the summer night back to our love nest."

His teasing hyperbole made her smile. "That sounds delightful. What time will you pick me up?"

"Well, if I were already staying here..." He trailed off, gauging her mood.

She pulled a robe out of her closet, slipped it on and belted it with a double knot. "You are incorrigible. Not tonight. Not tomorrow. Not this week. After the gala, we'll talk."

He pretended to scowl. "You're a hard woman."

She rounded the bed and slid her arms around his waist. "Patience, Hartley. That new house of yours will take weeks of work. We have all the time in the world."

Eleven

As it turned out, it was *Fiona* who was pressed for time. Not in regard to her work. She'd actually had bursts of energy in the late afternoons and was finding herself wildly productive in those moments. Although her workday had shifted and morphed from her usual pattern, she was not as far behind as she had feared.

The real problem was her clothes. When she dressed Wednesday morning, the jeans that had fit her only the day before were suddenly and mysteriously too tight. She stared in the mirror and ran a hand over her belly.

There was no denying it. Even if the convex shape of her tummy was barely perceptible to the naked eye, her body was changing. Blossoming with new life. The barrage of feelings that knowledge evoked made her feel completely out of her element.

She'd never had a mother, not really. What did she know about giving birth or breastfeeding or how many times was too many to read *Goodnight Moon*? Scarier still was wondering how her baby's father was going to react to the news. Would Friday night or perhaps Saturday morning be the right time to tell him? In the midst of her panic ran a deep, mysterious vein of intense joy.

Though this was a situation she had never anticipated or imagined she wanted, now that her baby was becoming a reality, she was fiercely glad. No matter what happened with Hartley, this child was *hers*. Hers. A family of her own.

In the end, she left her jeans unbuttoned at the waist and chose a loose cotton tunic in navy and orange that would hide any telltale signs. The appointment with her ob-gyn would confirm what she already knew.

Now she understood how Mazie felt the other day…slinking around, hoping no one would see. It was as if she had a giant sign on her back shouting, "I'm pregnant."

An hour later when a no-nonsense nurse called her name, Fiona rose to her feet and followed the woman through a maze of hallways to an exam room. The obstetrician was a female, only two or three years older than Fiona herself. Dr. Anderson was thorough, kind and reassuring. "You're in excellent health, Ms. James. You shouldn't have problems, but of course, you know to call our office immediately if you have any concerns."

The doc handed over a prescription for vitamins and a handful of educational pamphlets, and soon Fiona was out on the street again. She had been certain she was pregnant, but hearing the confirmation from a professional made everything so much more *real*.

As she stood on the sidewalk, her limbs were shaky, and her emotions pinballed. It was impossible to decide which response was the correct one. Jubilation and trepidation seemed equally appropriate.

Since she had already broken up her workday, she decided to consolidate errands. Before leaving the house that morning, she had looked online for maternity shops. There was one nearby, so she stopped in…just to take a look.

She had several tops at home that would probably work for three or four months. What she needed were some stretchy pants on the dressier side. Sometimes she met with prospective clients, so she had to look professional, even if she *was* an artist.

The clothing in this particular shop was wildly expensive, particularly considering she would be wearing maternity pieces for only part of a year. She found one sleeveless shift that she could wear over short-sleeve T-shirts. It didn't look like a tent, so that was a plus. A couple of pairs of pants and she was done for the moment.

It was hard to imagine her body getting big and round. Maybe it would be smarter to wait for the rest.

A more pressing priority than maternity clothes was finding something to wear for Friday night. She owned three relatively formal dresses, but none of them were really exciting. One was a hand-me-down from a friend. Another was the dress she'd worn at the wedding where she and Hartley met, and the third was a heavy winter velvet.

She wanted to look like she was comfortable in his world, even if she wasn't. Since this was definitely a special occasion, she sought out a little boutique where, normally, she only window-shopped. Today, she marched right in and started perusing the racks.

Sequins weren't really her thing. Color was another challenge. Black tended to overwhelm her because of her extremely fair skin and her stature. She wanted something *floaty* and romantic...the kind of gown a woman wore when going out with the man she loved.

The random thought stopped her dead in her tracks. She didn't *love* Hartley. She couldn't. Sexual attraction was a powerful force, but it wasn't the same as love.

Her stomach churned with nausea, though the baby wasn't to blame. For the first time, she honestly tried to imagine how Hartley was going to react when she told him the truth. She couldn't bear the thought that he would decide to care for her and the baby because he had no choice.

After being taken in by a string of well-meaning foster parents over the years of her childhood and adolescence, she'd had her fill of being someone else's *obligation*. She didn't need Hartley's money, and she didn't need his reluctant parenting.

He was worried about his mother's genetic legacy. Even more than that, his father had created such a mishmash of lies and deceit, Hartley was disgusted by the idea of parenthood. Hartley was determined not to recreate his unorthodox childhood. It made sense. It did. But there was absolutely nothing Fiona could do to alter the present situation. The only option would be to terminate the pregnancy, and that was out of the question.

This baby had already stolen her heart. Making plans for the future was scary and exciting at the same time. After the gala, she told herself. After the gala she would work up the courage to let Hartley know about her pregnancy. Who knows? Maybe the reality of her situation would change his mind.

"May I help you, miss?" A tall, statuesque saleswoman with exquisitely coiffed white hair interrupted Fiona's spate of worrying and gave her a warm smile.

"Yes, thank you. I have a function Friday night. Black-tie. Nothing I have at home will work. Can you point me in the right direction? I don't like anything too fussy, and I'd prefer the more casual side of formal. Am I asking the impossible? My hair clashes with some colors, obviously."

The woman took a step back and surveyed Fiona from head to toe, as if studying a mannequin. "White," she pronounced. "Possibly ivory, but I think white is the shade for you."

"Really? Isn't that a bit too bridal?"

"You must be attending the Chamber Awards Gala Friday, correct?"

"Yes, ma'am." It was hard not to feel like a little kid playing dress up when faced with this paragon of elegance.

"Come with me, young lady. The dressing rooms are this way. You may call me Clarisse."

Fiona trailed in her wake, wondering if she had started something she would regret. Even the changing area was fancier than her bedroom at home. A small antique chandelier. Tall cheval mirrors edged in gilt. Thick, lush carpet underfoot.

Clarisse indicated a small cushioned chair.

"Wait here," she said. "Help yourself to fruit water and biscotti."

When the other woman disappeared through plum satin curtains into the bowels of the store, Fiona sat down and pulled out her phone. She was increasingly worried about Hartley. After that first day, he had never again spoken about what he discovered in Switzerland.

Fiona was certain that if he simply told Jonathan the truth about why he had been gone and what he'd learned, his brother would no longer have a reason to be angry. Well, maybe because of the money, but Hartley had put it all back. That shouldn't be a problem in the end.

Clarisse returned with an armful of gowns, effectively ending Fiona's fretting, at least for the moment. The older woman ushered Fiona to a changing room. "Here are the first three," she said. "We can move on quickly if none of these suit your taste."

Fiona stripped down to her undies and surveyed the haul. One of the ivory dresses caught her eye instantly. It was strapless and fitted from the breasts to the knees, where it flared in a cloud of tulle. The satin had a faux antique patina that appealed to her artistic sensibilities.

But the fit was so tight...

She tried it on, holding her breath.

Clarisse rapped at the door. "Shall I zip you up?"

"Yes, please." Fiona couldn't tell anything at all with the dress open down the back. She clutched it to her chest and waited for the imperious salesclerk to help her.

When everything was tucked and fastened, both women surveyed Fiona's reflection in the glass. The woman looking back at them was wide-eyed and flushed.

Clarisse pursed her lips. "What do you think?"

Fiona touched her hair. Perhaps she could wear it up. "I love it," she said slowly, stunned that a single item of clothing could make her feel so wonderful. Already, she was imagining Hartley's face when he saw her in soft satin and bare skin. The dress made her feel sexy and sophisticated.

Clarisse nodded. "I believe it's perfect for you. But I suggest you try on half a dozen more just to be sure."

"Oh, no," Fiona demurred. "I won't change my mind, I promise. Are you sure I can pull this off? I'm not really accustomed to attending events like the gala. I don't want to feel self-conscious."

"If you're worried about the pregnancy showing, don't be. That tiny baby bump won't be visible at all, even though the dress fits as if it was designed only for you."

Fiona gaped. "You can tell I'm pregnant?" Her mood plummeted. "Maybe I should look for something looser."

Clarisse's expression softened. "I know women's bodies. It's my livelihood. But unless someone sees you naked, I assure you your secret is safe."

Unless someone sees you naked... Fiona gulped inwardly. Not exactly reassuring words given how the evening was likely to end. Hartley in a tux and Fiona dressed to kill? It was going to be their wedding party introduction all over again.

"I'll take the gown," Fiona said firmly. If she was going to be Hartley's plus-one and mingle with his family and friends and business acquaintances, she wanted to look her best.

After paying for her purchase and laying it gently in the back seat of the car, she pulled out her phone and did a search for Mazie's shop. It was a jewelry store in the historic district. As luck would have it, All That Glitters was less than a quarter of a mile away.

Fiona set out on foot. Parking spaces were at a premium in this part of town; plus, she needed the exercise anyway. Though she was by no means a slug, the fact that she was pregnant meant making healthy choices all the way around. She might be inexperienced when it came to babies and mothering, but she was determined to give this little one every advantage.

When she entered Mazie's place of business, the premises were pleasantly cool and scented with the aroma of jasmine. Quiet music played unobtrusively. Can lights overhead illuminated cases of rings and necklaces and bracelets. The atmosphere was everything a weary, overheated female tourist could hope for. Consequently, the place was crowded and buzzing with conversation.

Fiona spotted Hartley's sister right away, but she hung back, not wanting to intrude. When Mazie passed off a happy shopper to the employee at the register who was waiting to ring up and wrap the woman's purchases, Mazie made a beeline for Fiona.

She beamed. "You found me," she said.

"This place is gorgeous. I love how you've used color and light to showcase your merchandise."

"Thanks. Coming from an artist, that means a lot."

Fiona lowered her voice. "How are you feeling? What did J.B. say when he found out you're pregnant?"

The other woman's face was radiant. "I feel amazing. And my husband is over the moon. He barely lets me out of the house, though. Being doted on is great, but I've tried to tell him I'm fine."

"Maybe he'll settle down when he sees how well you're doing."

"I hope so. I love the attention—who wouldn't? Still, I need to breathe." Her smug smile told Fiona that J.B.'s hovering wasn't really a problem.

Mazie took her by the arm. "I need to talk to you," she said. Without waiting for a response from Fiona, she steered her toward the back of the store. "My office is tiny, but no one will disturb us."

Behind the chintz curtain was a jumble of

boxes and a nook barely large enough for an antique rolltop desk and a couple of chairs. Mazie motioned Fiona toward one of them. "Water?" she asked.

"Yes, please." The temperature was in the nineties. Her throat was dry. She was either nervous or dehydrated or both. "What's up?" she asked.

Mazie took the other seat and handed Fiona a bottle, then uncapped her own. "I'm worried sick about telling Lisette and Jonathan."

"And Hartley?"

"Him, too. But Lisette has miscarried twice. I don't want to upset her with my news."

"Don't be silly. You have something to celebrate. Lisette will be happy for you. She probably sees pregnant women every day."

"Maybe." Mazie wrinkled her nose. "J.B. and I thought that we'd have all of you over for drinks and hors d'oeuvres before the gala. That way we could tell everyone at once."

Mazie knew instantly this would be a test for her own pregnancy. If Hartley was delighted for his sister, maybe there was hope for Fiona. "We'll be there," she said.

"Excellent." Mazie hopped up and pulled a

small box from the shelf behind her shoulder. "I've been meaning to give you one of these," she said. "Sort of a welcome-to-the-family gift. It's clear that my brother is nuts about you."

Fiona wasn't sure this was the time to say that she and Hartley were temporary. So she smiled weakly and opened the offering. It was a delicate seahorse charm, suspended from a beautiful eighteen-inch box chain. "Oh, Mazie. This is lovely."

Mazie hovered. "Put it on. It's white gold. If you'd rather have the more traditional yellow, we can swap it out."

"Oh, no. This is perfect." Fiona fingered the little sea creature. "But I think it's too much. We barely know each other."

"You bought me pregnancy tests. That advances the timeline exponentially."

Fiona chuckled. "Maybe so." She stood and used the small oval mirror on the wall to fasten the chain around her neck. The charm nestled in exactly the right spot. "I love it."

"It's the kind of thing you can wear with everyday outfits. And it suits you. Whimsical and unusual."

"Are you sure that's a compliment?"

Fiona's wry question made Mazie laugh. "Of course it is. That's why my brother is so besotted. No woman he's ever dated is anything like you. You're an original."

"And all those other women?"

Mazie shrugged. "Cookie-cutter debutantes. Rich. Confident. Boring."

"We should all be so lucky," Fiona muttered. "I should go," she said suddenly, feeling weepy for no particular reason except that the life growing inside her was playing havoc with her temperament. "I just wanted to say hello and see where you worked."

"Well, now you know, so don't be a stranger."

When they returned to the main showroom, the crowd had thinned. Fiona wanted badly to share her own secret. But a host of things held her back. This family had a lot of skeletons. For an orphan, it was hard to imagine the kind of blood loyalty that kept a group of siblings together over the long haul.

"Thank you for the invitation," she said. "I'm sure Hartley will be happy for us to come." It wasn't exactly the truth, but she didn't want to add to Mazie's worry about the big reveal. "What time?"

"Probably five thirty. I'll text you both when we nail it down."

"You do realize it's only forty-eight hours from now?"

Mazie grinned. "Not to worry. I'll put my feet up and let J.B. make all the arrangements."

Twelve

Fiona continued to be sick in the mornings. Fitting into the dress she had bought was not a problem. Fortunately, Hartley kept his distance, perhaps hoping his uncustomary reticence would cement her trust.

For two days, it almost seemed as if time stood still. That she had never met Hartley. That her whole life wasn't about to change.

She took advantage of the momentary lull to paint like mad. The work was a welcome distraction. Anxiety about the weekend made her queasiness worse. She had agreed to spend the night with Hartley after the gala. In a romantic, indulgent boutique hotel. What could possibly go wrong?

At the wedding where they first met, and again when Hartley showed up at her house unannounced, the sex and the budding relationship had been wild and thrilling, carried along on a wave of lust and adrenaline and some insane concoction of pheromones.

Friday night would be different. She and Hartley were invited to socialize with his family. They were going to appear together in public. Neither of them could expect a spontaneous outcome. When a man and a woman dressed up, shared a fancy social occasion, and then checked into a room, what happened next was a done deal.

Fiona was both terrified and giddy with excitement.

In the end, she decided to leave her hair down. Her curls had a mind of their own, and they barely reached her chin. Taming them would take more energy than she possessed at the moment.

She was not a sophisticated woman. No point in pretending.

Friday afternoon she cleaned up her studio

and took a shower. She'd bought new undies and a silky nightgown at the maternity shop. Ordinarily, she was more of a tank top and panties sleeper, but tonight she wanted to be someone different. The kind of woman who coaxed a man into bed and made him never want to leave.

She and Hartley had texted back and forth over the past few days, but only briefly. Was he playing games with her? He'd gone from bludgeoning his way into her life to respecting her boundaries. What did it mean? Why was she so suspicious of his motives?

After packing a small overnight bag, she did her makeup and stepped into the fabulous dress. Only then did she realize her problem. With no Clarisse at hand, Fiona couldn't zip up the dress on her own.

Damn, damn, damn.

Hartley was as jumpy as a bullfrog on hot concrete. It felt like weeks, not days, since he had seen Fiona. He was playing the long game, giving her the space she wanted. Had it helped his case?

The only way he managed to survive his self-imposed separation was by working his ass off packing up his house and getting it ready for closing. All he could think about was whether or not Fiona was going to let him move in. Even if she made him sleep on the sofa, it would be a start. He'd made reservations at an extended-stay condo unit, just in case.

He had mixed feelings about showing up at J.B. and Mazie's house tonight. Lisette and Jonathan would be there, of course. Things were still frosty with his twin. Maybe avoidance was the best policy. Keep the width of the room between him and Jonathan.

Any worry about family squabbles took a back seat when Hartley pulled up in front of Fiona's now-familiar house. He shut off the engine, mentally calculating how many hours and minutes it would be until he and the lovely red-headed artist were alone together. His body tightened and ached as he imagined undressing her.

He had booked the best room in the swanki-est, most exclusive hotel in the city. Pulled out all the stops. Tonight would be a slow, sexy buildup to the main event.

If he lived that long. The way he felt right now, he might go quietly insane.

She knew they were good in bed. Why couldn't she admit the benefits of a convenient living arrangement?

He wanted her day and night.

Truth be told, his feelings for Fiona were not entirely comfortable, because he didn't understand them.

When he strode up the path and knocked, no one answered. Seconds passed. He knocked again. "Fiona, it's me."

Suddenly, he heard the sound of the dead bolt being turned. The door opened. But no more than six or eight inches. Certainly not enough for a large man to squeeze through.

Two big eyes in a heart-shaped face peered out at him. "You're early," she accused.

He frowned. "Barely fifteen minutes. What's wrong, Fee?"

The part of her he could see turned bright red. Perfect teeth mutilated a plump bottom lip. "We have a situation."

"Are you sick?" Disappointment flooded his stomach. And then he felt like a jerk for being disappointed.

"I'm not sick."

"Let me in, darlin'. It's hot enough to fry meat on the sidewalk."

"Okay. But wait a minute. And be quick when I let you in." The door closed all the way. Something—maybe an elbow—hit the wood.

He didn't know what the hell was going on, but he wasn't going to get any answers out here. "Fiona…"

Before he could form an objection, the door opened a second time. A small, feminine hand grabbed his wrist and dragged him through the narrow opening. "I need help," she said breathlessly.

When she slammed the door, and he saw her for the first time, he took a blow to the chest. His sweet, usually unadorned Fiona was wearing makeup. She looked unbelievably fantastic. Hot and sultry and gorgeous.

Her eye shadow was smoky gray, a color that made those slate blue irises sparkle. Mascara darkened pale lashes, creating a vision of feminine sexuality. She wore red lipstick, the color of arousal. His mouth dried. "You look amazing."

"Thank you. But I…"

Then he saw it. She was clutching her dress to her breasts. Ivory satin caressed her body. The gown appeared to be undone.

Lord help him.

Fiona's gaze was pleading. "The saleslady fastened me at the store. I never thought about the fact that I'd be home alone. You'll have to zip me up."

He took a step backward. Lust zinged from his sex to his throat, drying his mouth. "Um..."

"It's not a corset," she said. "Just a zipper." Impatience mixed with embarrassment in her voice.

He couldn't do it. He absolutely couldn't do it. All he'd thought about since the last time he stood in this house was how soon he could make love to her again. Now he was hot and horny and frustrated. Dangerously close to the edge. "A neighbor," he croaked. "I can fetch someone."

Confusion darkened her gaze. "Mr. Fontaine on the left is eighty-seven and deaf. My other neighbor has three kids, and they're at soccer practice. What's the problem? We're going to be late."

Well, hell. He could try. He wasn't a slave to

his baser instincts. He was a highly evolved, overly educated, twenty-first century gentleman.

She turned her back to him. "Do it, Hartley. Please."

Do it? Was she deliberately trying to drive him out of his mind?

His hands shook so hard he had to clench his fists. "Okay," he muttered. "Don't rush me. I don't want to ruin your dress."

Clearly, Fiona had no idea how she looked from behind. The zipper was a long one. Her soft, pale-skinned back was exposed from the nape of her neck to where her spine took a feminine curve at the top of her ass.

She wasn't wearing anything else but tiny underwear. And even then he got only a peek of lace. Mostly, the view was all Fiona. Naked Fiona.

Gritting his teeth, he took hold of the zipper and wrestled it upward an inch and a half, no more. Fiona made a noise that sounded remarkably like a moan.

He ignored the sexy provocation and tried again. The fabric was slippery. The dress was clearly meant to be fitted to a woman's body with little room to spare.

Suddenly, he had to touch her. Had to see if that magnolia-white skin was as soft as it looked. He traced her lower spine with both thumbs. "We could skip the gala tonight," he muttered, only half kidding.

Fiona shot him a look over her shoulder. "No, we can't." Her eyelids were heavy. The words lacked conviction.

He moved the zipper another inch. His self-control was shot. Wanting her was a living, breathing pain. How was he supposed to resist? He kissed the top of her spine. "Tell me to stop, Fee." His entire body was tense. Braced. As if being stretched on a rack. His sex throbbed beneath the confines of his tux pants.

"Stop what?"

It was a dangerous question, because in her voice he heard the truth. She knew exactly what he was asking.

"Fee…" He pleaded with her.

She dropped her head back against his chest, her curls brushing his chin. "I missed you," she muttered.

He snapped. Completely. His need for her

sent him reeling off a cliff. Without conscious thought, he lifted her bodily, freed her from the puddle of satin and kicked it aside.

Spinning her to face him, he ground out the only words he could think of in his delirium. "Speak now or forever hold your peace."

She curled her arms around his neck, her eyes soft with arousal. "I'm going to let you do all the talking," she whispered.

The madness rolled over him like a tide. He shoved her against the door, feasting on one perfect spot at the curve of her neck—careful, though, not to mark her skin. He freed his erection, fumbled with protection and fingered her sex through her panties. She was wet and warm and welcoming.

There was no time to remove her underwear. He tugged at the elastic between her legs and gave himself enough room to maneuver. Then he lifted her and shoved hard, lodging himself all the way to the hilt. Her butt smashed against the door.

Hell and damn. His body was on fire, burning from the inside out. When he moved in her, Fiona whimpered as if afraid he was going to leave her. Not bloody likely. "I'm sorry," he muttered. The weight of his many failings threatened to drown him. She was an angel, and he was nothing but a man enslaved by his need for her body, her soul.

Fee leaned into him and nipped his earlobe with sharp teeth. "I'm not sorry," she said.

Things blurred a bit after that. He remembered hammering into her again and again, muttering words of desperation. Fee's legs tightened around his waist. "Don't stop," she begged.

Half a second later, her sex contracted around his, the sensation exquisite and inescapable. He groaned her name and came with her, burying his hot face in her neck.

When it was over, he set her gently on her feet and kissed her forehead. He was weak, embarrassingly so. He couldn't think of a single thing to say.

Fiona, ever practical, touched his cheek, patting him as if he were a child to be comforted. "I'll use the bathroom in my studio. You can take the one in the hallway."

When she bent over to pick up her dress, he nearly lunged for her again. Instead, he clenched his fists and tried to breathe through the pain. He was falling in love with her. The knowledge crushed him. Fiona was the kind of woman who wanted marriage and a family.

He would give her the moon if she asked, but making babies was out of the question for him.

When he had put himself back together, at least where his clothing was concerned, he went to her bedroom and stood in the open doorway. Fee was seated at the antique vanity adjacent to her bed tidying her curls and freshening her lipstick. With her arms lifted and her body still naked, she looked like a painting by one of the old masters.

Woman combing her hair...

"Did I ruin your dress?" he asked. It was tossed across the bed.

"I don't think so." Her gaze didn't meet his when she stood. She hadn't bothered with slipping into a robe.

They were lovers. No need to pretend otherwise. Even so, he averted his eyes when she picked up the heavy satin and stepped into it. Too much temptation. She gave him her back. He zipped her up carefully.

"You look beautiful, Fiona." He squeezed her shoulders.

She had wrung him out and used him up, but he was hard as a pike already and wanted her no less than he had before.

"Thank you," she said quietly. "We should go. We can still make it to Mazie and J.B.'s if the traffic is kind." She picked up a small evening clutch covered in seed pearls.

"Wait," he said, reaching into the pocket of his jacket. "I almost forgot. Mazie told me the two of you chatted when you stopped by the store about what you were going to wear tonight. I pumped her for the color and bought you this. I hope you like it."

He handed over a velvet box and watched her face as she opened it.

Her eyes widened. "Hartley...these are gorgeous. But it's too much. I'd be terrified of breaking them."

"Nonsense. Pearls are meant to be enjoyed. They warm with your skin...become part of you. Turn around."

Carefully, he slipped the long double strand over her head. The woman and the dress had been stunning before. Now Fiona looked like a princess. He stood behind her as she examined her reflection in the mirror. Their eyes met in the glass. "I love them," she said. "Thank you, Hartley." When she stroked the necklace with two fingers, he could almost feel her touch against his skin.

He swallowed against a startling lump of emotion in his throat. "I'm glad. I would kiss you, but I don't think we have time for more repairs."

Fiona glanced at the clock on her bedside table and squeaked. "We have to go. Mazie will kill us if we're late."

"What's so important?" He loved his sister, but he was more interested in being alone with Fiona than a round of appetizers and small talk.

Fiona's cheeks turned pink. "Who knows? Your siblings are complicated people."

"So true." While Fee turned off lights and checked doors, Hartley took her small suitcase and put it in the trunk of his car. Only the fact that they were spending the night together kept him in line. It would be far too easy to blow off this gala and let Mazie and Jonathan represent the family.

Truth be told, he still felt guilty about leaving them to do that the whole time he'd been gone. He'd borne a load of his own, but did that balance out the sin of abandoning the family?

In the car, he took Fiona's hand and lifted it to his lips. "Thank you for coming with me tonight. I'll be the most envied man in Charleston with you on my arm."

When he nibbled her knuckles, she jerked her hand back, laughing. "Behave yourself. And don't think ridiculous flattery will let you have your way about everything."

"It's only flattery if it isn't true, Fee. I'm not sure how a woman like you is still unattached."

His praise seemed to bother her. She wrinkled her nose and stared through the windshield. "What does that mean? A woman like me..."

He started the car. "Beautiful. Smart. Talented. Sexy as hell."

"I appreciate the vote of confidence, but I'm not anything special. Don't get me wrong. I have healthy self-esteem. I'm not fishing for compliments."

"Then what *are* you doing?" He frowned, bothered by the fact that she seemed clueless about how she affected him.

"Let's change the subject, please."

He bowed to her wishes, wondering how deeply her early years had marked her. What was it like to be a kid without a home? He couldn't even imagine it.

Yet, he'd *had* a home, and he possessed as many hang-ups as Fiona. Perhaps more. Warning bells sounded in his head. He was getting in too deep. He didn't need to psychoanalyze her to enjoy sex. He needed to back up and look at the big picture.

Fiona was silent for the remainder of the short trip. As always, he wondered what she was thinking. Was she looking forward to sleeping with him tonight? Really sleeping? He was vaguely astonished to realize that he wanted that almost as much as he wanted sex.

Maybe this relationship was temporary. In his gut, he knew it was. That didn't mean he couldn't enjoy it while it lasted.

Thirteen

Fiona was a pile of nerves by the time she and Hartley made it to Mazie's house. The two of them were a full ninety seconds early, a minor miracle considering how they had spent portions of the previous hour.

A uniformed maid met them at the door and escorted them to the dining room. The home was stunning. But Fiona had no time to gawk at the classic architecture and fabulous furnishings. Everyone else was already present. Jonathan and Lisette. And of course, J.B. and Mazie.

Hartley hadn't lost all of his reserve with his siblings. The round of greetings was cordial, but to Fiona's eyes, everyone in the room was carefully on his or her best behavior. She exchanged hugs, too... That seemed to be required. Only Jonathan and Hartley kept a physical distance.

The light appetizers set out on the sideboard were amazing. Fiona could have made a meal out of only this, but she worried about spilling food on her dress. Given how careless she had been with her beautiful new gown already, perhaps she shouldn't press her luck.

When everyone had been wined and dined, J.B. commanded the floor. Fiona expected Mazie to make the big announcement. Instead, her husband grinned widely.

"We're glad you came tonight. Mazie thought this would be a good time to get us all together."

Jonathan looked puzzled. "We're going to the gala—sitting at the same table. I'm not sure what you mean."

Mazie patted her husband's arm and nodded. She glowed. Apparently, that was a real thing. Except for the unfortunate ones like Fiona who were sick as dogs.

J.B. laid a hand on his wife's shoulder. The two of them exchanged a private look that was intimate and smug with happiness. Then J.B., former bad boy and now thoroughly content homebody, cleared his throat. "We're pregnant," he said. "Well, Mazie is. We wanted you all to know."

After a moment of stunned silence, Lisette was the first one to react. She jumped to her feet and smiled broadly. "That's wonderful news. I'm thrilled for you."

Mazie stood as well and embraced her sister-in-law. "I wasn't sure what to say to you, Lizzy. You and Jonathan have been disappointed twice. I feel guilty that I'm the one who's pregnant."

Lisette shook her head slowly. "Silly goose. Your happiness doesn't hurt me. Jonathan and I are fine. We don't know what the future holds for us, but we'll be tickled pink to welcome the first of a new generation of Tarletons."

"And Vaughans," J.B. said. "Don't forget the daddy."

In the midst of laughter and more hugging, Fiona sneaked a sideways glance at Hartley. He was saying and doing all the right things, but he was pale beneath his tan. Had his family noticed? They had all known him far longer than Fiona had. Maybe it was her imagination.

Jonathan picked up a flute of champagne from the sideboard. "To new beginnings," he said. "And to a healthy pregnancy and a perfect little baby—" He halted, an arrested look on his face. "Boy? Girl?"

"Too soon to tell," Mazie said. "Plus, there's always the possibility of multiples given the meds I've taken."

J.B. turned green. "Oh, hell," he muttered. "I forgot about that."

Mazie slid her arm around his waist and chuckled. "I wondered how long it would take you to remember."

Lisette glanced at her watch. "I hate to break up the party, but if we're going to make it in time for the presentation, we'd better head out."

Jonathan nodded. "You're right, sweetheart. One more thing, though. I'll make it quick." When everyone fell silent, Jonathan stared at his twin with a hard-to-read expression.

Fiona had sat down again on the sofa. Hartley perched on the arm beside her. She felt the fine tension in his body when Jonathan spoke.

The CEO of Tarleton Shipping addressed the

room. His brown-eyed gaze, so like his sibling's, was focused on his brother. "We've all been through a lot in the past year. Changes and more changes. But one thing stays the same… family." The muscles in his throat worked visibly. "I want you to come back to work, Hartley. The company needs you. I need you. Whatever happened while you were away is water under the bridge. The important thing now is that you've come home."

Fiona was stunned. She squeezed Hartley's hand, silently urging him to accept the olive branch.

He stood up slowly. She had no idea what he was thinking. "I'd like that," he said gruffly. He reached out to his brother. "Thanks, Jonathan."

All the women were misty-eyed as the two men shook hands. There wasn't time to dwell on the tentative truce. Maybe Jonathan planned it that way. Everyone rushed to gather phones and car keys and purses.

Soon, Fiona was in the car with Hartley. "Well, *that* was awesome," she said. "I'm so happy for you."

When Hartley didn't respond, she put a hand on his shoulder briefly. "You okay?" she asked as she fastened her seat belt, taking care not to clip the delicate fabric of her dress in the mechanism.

Hartley pulled out into traffic, his big hands clenched around the steering wheel. "I'm fine." His jaw was granite hard.

"I don't think you are. I thought you'd be excited about returning to Tarleton Shipping."

"I'm pleased," he said tersely. The declaration was hard to believe.

Fiona chewed her lip. "No one is holding a grudge. No one is demanding answers about why you were gone. Your family is wonderfully intact."

"Maybe," he muttered. "He was my best friend. I doubt we'll ever get that back."

"Which is why you have to tell them the truth. You see that...right? Jonathan and Mazie need to know that their mother is not their mother. And that you didn't abandon them for no good reason. This is a critical time for your sister."

Hartley muttered a rude word beneath his breath. "Ignorance is bliss. Trust me on this."

"You are so damned stubborn," she cried. His intractability infuriated her. But they were already pulling up at the event site, so she had to drop the argument.

Crowds of impeccably dressed attendees poured into the building. The venue had once been a trio of row houses. Careful renovation turned the historic structure into an upscale, sophisticated spot for weddings and other special occasions.

Tonight, the chamber of commerce was celebrating philanthropy in Charleston and honoring Gerald Tarleton with a posthumous award. He would have received the honor in person had he not died so unexpectedly.

As guests entered the building and gathered in a large, bright atrium, screens on four walls detailed the many programs and projects to which the Tarleton patriarch had been a benefactor. The photographs spanned a couple of decades. From the older images, it was easy to see that Jonathan and Hartley resembled their father in his younger days.

The chamber president quieted the crowd and summoned the three Tarleton siblings to the miniature dais. J.B., Lisette and Fiona lingered at the back of the room.

For the first time, Fiona truly understood the

place this family held in the story of the port city. The Tarletons were low-country royalty. She was glad all the focus was on the stage. She felt queasy and out of her element.

Hartley was so damned sexy when he stepped up to the microphone and said a few words. She put a hand to her chest to still the ache there. She was such a hypocrite...insisting that he come clean about his trip to Europe. Insisting that secrets were hurtful.

Soon, the brief ceremony was over and huge double doors swung inward, allowing the crowd to progress to the ballroom where a fancy meal was waiting. When the Tarletons rejoined their respective partners, Fiona felt even more like a fraud. She was here under false pretenses. Hartley wanted her. He'd said so in a dozen different ways.

But their fledgling relationship wouldn't stand a chance when the truth came out.

The large room filled rapidly with conversation and laughter. The waiters and waitresses who moved between tables were a welcome distraction. Hartley was seated beside her, but he felt a thousand miles away.

Despite the intimacy he and Fiona had shared

earlier, he was only going through the motions now. Behind his pleasant smile she saw a world of confusion. He was hurting, and she didn't know how to help him.

Who was she kidding? She didn't even know how to help herself.

Though the food was wonderful, she ate sparingly. She still had to get through the early morning hours without revealing her *interesting* condition. As much as she wanted to spend the night with Hartley, she was courting danger.

Tomorrow, she wanted to tell him calmly, rationally. Not have him find out about the baby because she was hunched over the toilet losing her breakfast.

Things improved when the lights dimmed and couples began moving onto the dance floor in the center of the room. Crystal chandeliers overhead reflected candle flames from the ornate centerpieces.

Hartley stood and held out his hand. "Dance with me?" he asked gruffly. When she twined her fingers with his, he tugged her to her feet.

"I'd love to," she said.

Hartley was an amazing dancer. She remembered that from the wedding where they met. Though he was big and broad and unabashedly masculine, he moved with confidence across the polished floor.

When she tried to keep a space between them, Hartley simply ignored her self-conscious behavior. "No one's watching us," he said, his breath warm on her temple. "Relax, Fee."

She was pretty sure he was deluding himself. A good portion of the room—at least the single females from twenty to forty—were eyeing Hartley like he was dark chocolate and they had just finished a ten-day juice cleanse.

Hartley, on the other hand, was flatteringly single-minded. He held her close. His gaze never strayed to other women. His beautiful cognac eyes mesmerized her.

"This is fun," she said, resting her cheek against his shoulder. It wasn't what she *wanted* to say. She wanted to pour out her thoughts and her fears and her questions about the future. She wanted to tell him how he made her life brighter and better. How he made her feel desirable and sexy and *hopeful*.

She wanted to tell him she loved him. Her

breath hitched. The knowledge had come to her gradually, but could no longer be ignored.

The words lodged in her throat. Like Cinderella watching the clock, Fiona didn't want to miss a single moment of the magic. She was racing against time, trying desperately to see a solution where there was none.

She *knew*, deep in her heart, that as soon as she revealed the truth about her pregnancy, Hartley would be long gone and she would turn into a fat orange pregnant pumpkin with nothing to show for this crazy affair other than a single glass slipper and a broken heart.

J.B. and Mazie were the first to leave the party. Like Fiona, Mazie had been battling exhaustion. Jonathan and Lisette soon followed.

As the room emptied, Hartley and Fiona remained on the dance floor, swaying from one romantic song until the next. Earlier in the evening, the band had played pop tunes. Top-forty hits.

Now, with the lights low and only two dozen couples still enjoying the music, the old standards were the best. Especially as a prelude to a cozy overnight rendezvous at a nearby hotel.

Hartley stroked the back of her neck with a

single fingertip, reducing her to a puddle of need. "I want you, Fee."

The hoarse words were not surprising. He'd been noticeably aroused for the past hour. She tipped back her head and searched his face. "I want you, too," she said softly. *So. Very. Much.*

They gathered their things from the table and headed for the exit. Numerous people interrupted their progress to say something to Hartley about his father, but finally, they were out on the street in the warm, muggy heat of a Charleston evening.

Hartley had parked the car in a two-tiered garage around the corner from the venue. They strolled there slowly, hands linked like teenagers on prom night. Despite everything that was wrong, Fiona experienced a totally illogical surge of hope.

Maybe Hartley did care for her more deeply than she thought.

Maybe he would be able to handle her shocking news with equanimity.

Maybe she would finally have the family she had always wanted.

At the car, Hartley insisted on carrying both bags. He tucked his smaller case under his arm and picked up Fiona's carry-on. "I'm still holding your hand," he said, giving her his trademark grin. "Tonight is a big romantic gesture. I'm impressing you with my strength and stamina."

She bumped his hip with hers. "Save the stamina for later."

His cheeks flushed. "Duly noted."

Their lodging was a brief walk away. The streets were mostly deserted. When they arrived, a sleepy desk clerk checked them in. Hartley had booked the rooftop suite with a view of the city.

They skipped the elevator and climbed three flights of stairs. Since her escort had his hands full, Fiona unlocked the door and walked in. "Oh, Hartley," she said, delighted. "This is gorgeous." The furnishings were soft and stylish but not too over-the top for a man to feel comfortable. A deep, inviting sofa upholstered in sage green suggested any number of alternatives for adult play. The huge four-poster bed dominated the room.

Beyond the bed, French doors opened outward onto a private patio. Fee kicked off her shoes and went to explore. When Hartley dropped the bags and followed her outside, she leaned over the railing. "This place is perfect."

He wrapped his arms around her waist from behind, tugging her back from the edge. *"You're perfect."*

The absolute sincerity in his voice wooed her, turned her knees to mush. She spun to face him. "Thank you, Hartley. Thank you for thinking of this."

He kissed her nose. "Sit right there. Don't move." The small table was flanked by two metal chairs.

Moments later, he was back carrying a bottle of champagne and two glasses. "This was our welcome gift."

As he started to work on the cork, Fiona felt panic rise. Pregnant women couldn't drink. "None for me," she said. "I want to be awake for the next act. But you have some."

He gazed at her quizzically, setting the bottle aside. "Whatever the lady wants."

She reached across the table and took his hand. "I'll ask it again. Are you okay?"

His expression altered for a split second and then settled back into his habitual lazy grin. Had she touched a nerve?

"Why wouldn't I be?" he said, but his fingers drummed on the table.

"We haven't had a chance to discuss your sister's news. I was afraid it upset you."

His jaw worked visibly. The silence lengthened. "I don't think it's *good* news, if that's what you're asking. But before you start in on me, it wouldn't have changed anything if I had told them the truth. They wanted a baby. Mazie already knows that mental illness runs in our family."

Fiona sighed inwardly. Had she ever met a more stubborn man? "Genetics is a tricky business," she said. "Besides, their baby is half Vaughan. None of us can guarantee a perfect pregnancy ahead of time. It's a roll of the dice."

"Good thing I'm not a gambler."

She glared at him, completely frustrated, but unable to tell him why.

Suddenly, Hartley stood up and paced. "Do you really want to have this argument right now? I thought we were here to indulge ourselves."

He was right. Once she told him the truth tomorrow morning, everything would change. She wanted this one last night. She wanted

Hartley. The other could wait. "I'm sorry," she said. She mimed locking her lips and tossing the keys. "From now on, it's all about you and me."

At last, his body language relaxed. "I'm glad to hear it." He moved behind her chair and played with her hair, sifting the strands, his fingers brushing her ears, making her tremble. He had barely touched her, and already she was wild for him.

When she tried to stand up, two big hands settled on her shoulders. "Don't move, darlin'. We're gonna take this slow. We have all night."

It was supposed to be a promise on his part, but to her ears, it sounded dangerous. *All night*? What was she thinking? Morning always came, and with it, a reckoning.

He reached around her and slid his slightly rough man-hands inside the bodice of her dress, cupping her bare curves. She shuddered, biting her lip to hold back a ragged moan. Sounds carried on the night air.

"What are you doing?" she whispered.

"Enjoying myself." The laughter in his voice made her smile, though she was too wound for amusement to take hold.

She exhaled shakily. "Carry on."

He played with her breasts, making her squirm. The nipples were more sensitive now that she was pregnant. When he kissed her neck and nuzzled the spot just below her ear—because he knew she liked it—she reached up and grabbed his wrists. "I want to go inside," she pleaded.

"Not yet." Without warning, he tugged her to her feet. "Let's look at the stars."

Fourteen

Fiona was confused. They were outside. All they had to do was look up. Apparently, that wasn't enough for Hartley. He tugged her toward the edge of the patio where a low stone wall topped with three feet of wrought iron marked a boundary. A century and a half ago, a gentleman might have coaxed a Southern belle up here to see the sights.

The hour was late. Few people roamed the streets below. The ones who did, didn't look up.

Hartley stood behind her, crowding her. "Hold on, Fee." He took her hands and placed them on the smooth, cool metal curlicues. "Don't let go."

Her heart beat faster. Could he see the way

her chest rose and fell with her startled breathing? She wanted to question him, to demand an explanation. But another part of her, submissive, aroused, wanted to see how far this would go. Hartley was a modern-day pirate. An adventurer. A man unafraid to push the bounds of propriety.

Even so, she was shocked beyond words when she felt him lift her skirt. Despite the season and the temperature, the air felt cool on her bare legs and the backs of her thighs. "Hartley?" The ragged word was equal parts protest and slurred pleasure. Surely he wouldn't...

Once again, he kissed the back of her neck. "I'll keep you safe, sweet thing. You can trust me."

Her fingers clenched painfully around the unforgiving iron. She might have swooned had twenty-first-century women been given permission to do such a girly thing.

His big hands palmed her butt, squeezing. He made no move to take off her panties, but his thumb traced the crease in her ass through nylon and lace. Goose bumps covered her body.

Her voice was frozen, her breath lodged in her throat. Between her legs, her sex wept for him. She was swollen and hot and damp, unbearably needy. Would he unzip her dress? Here, where they were exposed?

The idea both frightened and seduced her.

Hartley continued to play with her backside as if he had all the time in the world. Just when she thought she couldn't bear another second of his lazy torture, he reached around her and, with a single finger, stroked her to a sharp, vicious climax. She shuddered and groaned.

Afterward, her forehead rested against the metal. She could barely breathe. His hand was concealed by layers of tulle and satin. If anyone on the street below was inclined to gaze upward, nothing would seem amiss.

Hartley moved closer. She felt his arousal at her back. "I told you we'd see stars," he muttered, his voice heavy.

Her body went lax, leaned into his. But still, she held the railing. "How much did you have to drink, Hartley Tarleton? You're out of control."

His laughter was strained. "Possibly." He covered her hands with his.

The visual was enticing and beautiful and painfully perfect. She wanted this man and this life. But she wanted more. She wanted a future full of love and laughter and family squabbles. She wanted everything.

Without warning, he scooped her into his arms. "I'd like to get horizontal now. Any objections?"

Fiona waved a hand, yawning. "Not a single one."

Hartley knew he had met his match. There had never been a female he couldn't walk away from. Not until Fee.

Lust and tenderness and determination swirled in a dangerous cocktail of emotion. He wanted this woman. Maybe forever. The knowledge should have stunned him, but oddly, he recognized it. The need to claim her as his own had been growing underground. He'd told himself he was having fun.

Instead, he'd been making plans.

Fiona had no family of her own. He could share his.

As he carried her over the threshold into their hedonistic bedroom and bumped the door closed with his hip, his heart beat faster, a syncopated rhythm that made him breathe too fast.

Was there more to this thing with Fee than sex? Did he want more?

Now they were enclosed in a cool, private lovers' boudoir that smelled of roses and sin. He set her on her feet and kissed her roughly, his hands tangling in her hair, holding her head.

"I never seem to get enough of you, Fiona. Why do you think that is?"

Her sleepy smile was sweet and guileless. "I have no idea. But I'm a fan of your work."

His hands shook. "I may not be able to stop. I may have to take you all night, again and again. Like that first time we met."

"Do you hear me complaining?"

The sass in her voice inflamed him. Something about this weekend was bringing out his caveman instincts. He backed her up against the carved post at the foot of the bed. Falling to his knees, he knelt between her legs and found his way under her skirt.

Her skin was hot and fragrant with a familiar scent. He nudged her feet apart. Though his body ached fiercely with the need to be inside her, he wanted to give her every ounce of pleasure possible.

When he tasted her intimately, she groaned.

Her hands fisted in his hair, making him wince. This time, her orgasm was slower, richer. It rolled over both of them in an endless stream. Hartley felt the quivers in her pelvis, the sharp jerk when her body hit the top.

She collapsed in his arms. He eased her down onto the soft, luxurious rug, wrapping her tightly against him. While Fee struggled to breathe, he pressed kisses to her hot face. "I need you, Fiona James. Tell me you want me, too."

"Of course I do." She blinked at him, befuddled.

"What if we travel the world for a few months? Give you new horizons and inspirations to paint? We'll go wherever the wind blows us."

She flinched. The change in her face was so obvious a blind man would have seen it. While Hartley had been weaving dreams, Fiona had clearly been on a different track. Distress darkened her soft blue-gray eyes. "Your brother asked you to come back to work. You can't abandon him again."

Suddenly, he remembered Fiona's aversion to his spending the night at her house. What kind of fool was he? A woman who wanted her "space" clearly wasn't keen on spending a lot of time together.

The raw hurt in his chest was astounding. Had he really been so clueless about his own obsession and Fiona's ambivalence?

"Forget I said anything," he said lightly, tucking away the heartsick feeling in his gut. "It was the lust talking. You're a very sexy woman. I plead temporary insanity."

"Hartley..." She cupped his face.

He'd be damned if he'd let her see that she had bruised his ego. Jumping to his feet, he dragged her with him. "Enough talking," he muttered.

He stripped the dress and underwear from her body and then removed his own clothes rapidly. After folding back the sumptuous covers, he tumbled her onto the bed. He wanted to prove to himself that his emotions weren't involved.

But when he tried to be rough and impersonal like this was just another encounter with just another nameless female, he couldn't do it. Fee's bottom lip trembled. Her beautiful eyes welled with tears. "I care about you, Hartley. You know I do."

The lukewarm words were like alcohol on a razor cut. He held her wrists in one hand and loomed over her. "Let's put that to the test."

Deliberately, he held her down and pleasured her, made her come three times. Every time she tried to coax him to enter her, he resisted... even though the truth was, he was sick with wanting her.

Finally, his body betrayed him. He'd been aroused for a million hours, desperate to find solace in her arms, her soft, sweet body. He spread her legs and thrust hard, finding himself at the mouth of her womb, buried as deeply as he could go. Wanting to bind her to him. To demand that she acknowledge this incredible connection they shared.

It was over soon. Humiliatingly so.

He visited the bathroom. So did she. After turning out the lights, they climbed into bed. It would have been a fitting end to the evening if he could have turned his back on her. But he was weak in the way only a man could be. He dragged her close and spooned her, already yawning.

They fell asleep without another word.

* * *

Fiona awoke at dawn, groggy and needing to pee. It took a moment for her surroundings to register. And then she remembered. The hotel. Hartley.

Panic struck as she assessed her nausea. Unbelievably, her stomach was at rest. Maybe she was turning the corner. It didn't matter anymore, though, did it? Hartley would have to be told about the baby today, and then it was all over.

When she turned on her side to look at him, his eyes were open. He was on his back, arm slung over his forehead, staring at the ceiling.

"What do you want to do?" she asked. They had made plans to enjoy brunch, play tourist at the open-air market, spend a second night at the hotel, make love until they were satisfied.

Hartley didn't even look at her. "I think we should check out of the room. Head home. Separately. We need to back up and take a look at what we're doing. You're right, Fiona. If I'm returning to work at Tarleton Shipping right away, I'll have a lot on my plate."

"You're angry," she said, her heart sinking.

He shrugged. "No."

It was time for the truth. She sat up and wrapped the sheet around her all the way up to her neck. This wasn't an easy conversation to have naked. "I need to tell you something," she whispered.

Shivers racked her body. The nausea threatened to return.

Without warning, Hartley rolled out of bed. "I'm done with talking and listening, Fee. I'm calling a time-out. You in your corner. Me in mine. This relationship is too damn much work."

The next thirty minutes passed in a haze of misery. They took turns showering. Room service sent up coffee and croissants. When both Hartley and Fiona were dressed and ready to go, they carried their bags downstairs and turned in the keys. Fiona's overnight case held a satin gown folded up inside.

Hartley drove her home without speaking a word. He stopped at her sidewalk and left the motor running. There was no choice but to get out, yet something held her back. "Are you done with me?" she asked. "Done with us?"

His expression was inscrutable. "I don't know."

* * *

In the days that followed, Fiona lost herself in her work. It was a pattern that had served her well in the past. She felt the urgency of getting all her large commissions finished before the baby came. What did she have? Five months? Six? Babies could come early or late…

She had no idea how she would cope in the beginning. Caring for a newborn was a huge amount of work. And there would be no paid maternity leave for a self-employed artist.

Should she swallow her pride and ask for Hartley's help? He must have thought his travel-the-world plan hadn't interested her. Quite the opposite. It sounded like the most amazing honeymoon.

But preparing for the baby and getting her projects completed didn't leave any time for a months-long jaunt.

And still she hadn't told her baby's father the truth. Though it wasn't entirely her fault, she felt guilty. The longer she waited, the harder it seemed, particularly after the way their romantic weekend had ended.

Despite her distress over the way she and Hartley had parted and her worry about the future, each day brought new reasons to be excited about her pregnancy. Thankfully, she had made it through the worst of the morning sickness. It still caught her off guard at times, but not every day and not as badly as before.

Her breasts were bigger now. The little baby bump was growing more noticeable. Slowly but surely, her body was changing. Soon, telling Hartley would be a moot point. People would begin to notice her shape and draw their own conclusions.

Every morning she told herself today was the day. She would seek him out, give him the news and weather the explosion. After all, this baby linked them, no matter what. But every day she lost her nerve. Seeing the look on his face when he heard the truth would destroy her.

She *wanted* this baby. Desperately. Knowing that Hartley couldn't or *didn't* broke her heart.

Over a week after the gala, Mazie showed up unannounced on Fiona's doorstep. Because she was working, Fiona nearly didn't answer the bell. But her back was hurting, and she needed a break anyway.

She wiped her hands, peeked through the window and felt her heart catch with disappointment. It wasn't Hartley. Of course it wasn't.

Fiona opened the door. "Hey, Mazie. What's up? Come on in. Please excuse the fact that I'm covered with paint. Neatness is not one of my gifts."

Mazie tossed her keys in a chair and put her hands on her hips. Her usual sunny smile was nowhere in sight. "What have you done to Hartley?" She demanded an answer.

The pile of guilt smothering Fiona grew deeper. "Nothing," she said weakly. "I don't know what you mean." She wrapped her arms around her waist, feeling her face heat.

Hartley's sister paced, her stance agitated. "Jonathan is worried about him. He says things are going smoothly at work, but Hartley is distant."

"Well, that makes sense, doesn't it? You're all dealing with the fallout from his being gone. I'm sure it will take some time to get back to the way things were. I wouldn't worry about it."

"That's not all." Mazie scowled, her expression stormy and anxious at the same time. "J.B. is throwing a big party for my birthday soon. I asked Hartley to bring you, and he gave me some weird evasive answer about how you were super busy. It was clearly a lie. What's going on with you two?"

In another circumstance, Fiona might have confessed her pregnancy. She liked Mazie and felt close to her already. But to admit she was pregnant would bring a host of questions and problems. Mazie would rightly want to know why Fiona hadn't told Hartley he was going to be a father—and why Fiona and Hartley weren't living together.

Fiona couldn't explain any of that without divulging Hartley's secrets.

Those secrets weren't hers to tell.

"I'm sure Hartley can find a date for the birthday party. And I'm also sure it's not good for the baby *or* you to get so upset. Give Hartley some space and time to regroup. He'll be fine."

Mazie cocked her head, studying Fiona as if she could see inside her brain. "I was under the impression the two of you were pretty serious."

Fiona bit her lip. Hard. She refused to cry in front of the other woman. "I think Hartley and I want different things out of life. Besides, he needs a chance to get back in the groove at Tarleton Shipping."

"Did you have a fight?"

How was Fiona supposed to answer that? "Not a fight *exactly*. I suppose you could say we had words. But it's over. We're both fine."

Mazie scrunched up her face and ran her hands through her hair. "Why can't anything be simple, dammit? I thought you were perfect for my brother. I can't believe he let you slip through his fingers."

"It was my fault," Fiona said, not wanting Mazie to be disappointed in her brother. "I needed things that Hartley wasn't ready to give. So don't blame him. It's just that he and I are two very different people."

Mazie's face fell. "Well, that sucks. Can you tell me more? Maybe I can knock some sense into him."

"It's personal," Fiona said. "I'm sorry, Mazie. I love your family, and I would have liked to be a part of it. But it's not in the cards." She paused briefly. "I hate to be rude, but I really do need to get back to work."

Mazie's eyes glittered with tears. "He needs somebody."

"You're matchmaking, because you and J.B. are so happy, but not every relationship works out. Hartley will find someone else." Saying those words out loud was an actual physical pain.

"I suppose." Mazie's glum acceptance didn't make Fiona feel any better at all. "I still wish you could come to my birthday party," Mazie said.

"Perhaps you and I should have lunch one day. Just the two of us. A girl can never have too many friends."

"I'd like that. I won't let you slip away simply because my brother is dumb. I'll call you soon. Sorry to interrupt your work."

Fiona said her goodbyes, locked the front door, threw herself down on the sofa and cried…

Fifteen

Unfortunately, tears never solved anything. When her pity party was over, she was no closer than ever to finding answers, and now she had a headache and a stuffy nose besides.

She wiped her face with the hem of her T-shirt and sat up. Reaching in her pocket for her phone before she could change her mind, she sent Hartley a text.

I miss you.

When he didn't answer right away, she reminded herself that he was at work. The important thing was, she had made an overture. Not only did he need to come pick up his birthday gift for his sister, but Fiona needed to see him face-to-face and tell him the truth.

To make sure she didn't back out again, she added a second text.

Mazie's birthday present is ready. Let me know when you want to pick it up.

The dizziness and light-headed feeling she experienced when she hit Send had nothing to do with her pregnancy this time. She was so damned scared.

What would she do if he ignored her entirely? Thankfully, Mazie's painting was Fiona's ace in the hand.

A few hours later as she was fixing herself an early dinner of tomato soup and grilled cheese, her phone finally dinged. Now is good for me, the text said.

Her heart stopped. She wasn't ready. Her hands were clammy and shaky.

Can we make it 6:30?

I'll be there.

With barely an hour to scarf down her food, clean up the kitchen and take a quick shower, she had to hurry. Instead of a sundress, which was her go-to hot-weather wardrobe when she wanted to look nice, she found a pair of new jeans in her closet and paired them with a simple button-up shirt. White. Sleeveless. Nothing to say she wanted to look good in front of an ex-lover.

For courage, she added the seahorse pendant Mazie had given her. The little creature was cool against her hot skin.

Again and again she rehearsed the words she wanted to say when she revealed her pregnancy. All the things she had wanted to say when they were at the hotel but didn't have the chance. Letting Hartley off the hook. Telling him he didn't have to be involved with the baby at all.

All the practice in the world wasn't going to make this confrontation any less painful. What she really wanted to do was get down on her knees and beg him to love her *and* her baby. To plead with him to be happy.

When the knock came at six thirty sharp, she opened the door. Instantly, she knew that Mazie had been right. Hartley looked terrible.

Still handsome, of course, but stripped of life. His eyes were dull. The usual joie de vivre that put a twinkle of mischief in his expressive face was gone.

"Come on in," she said. "The painting is on the sofa."

When she closed the door, he stopped in front of her and bent to kiss the top of her head. "Hello, Fee."

Silly tears sprang to her eyes. She blinked them away. His tenderness was more painful than outright hostility. Swallowing the huge lump in her throat, she led him through to the living room. "There it is."

Hartley stopped in his tracks, his expression awed. "My God, Fiona. This is phenomenal." He picked up the small canvas with careful hands and examined it closely. "You've captured the two of them exactly. Mazie will adore it." He turned back to look at her, where she had paused in the doorway. "I knew you were talented, but this is something else again. You're an amazing artist. I don't think I fully understood how gifted you are until now."

His praise warmed the cold places in her broken heart. "Thanks. I'm happy you like it. Shall

I wrap it for you?" She had brought the supplies from her studio just in case.

"Yes, please."

He prowled the room for the few minutes it took her to enfold the framed canvas in thick kraft paper and tie it with a fancy golden bow. "There you go," she said. "All ready for the birthday girl." Some tiny part of her still expected him to invite her to the party, but Hartley didn't say a word.

Despite the awkwardness between them, a silly sprig of hope continued to push through her fear. She couldn't procrastinate any longer. "Hartley, I need to talk to you about something."

"Me first," he said. "I need a favor. I know we didn't part on the best of terms, but I need your help."

"With what?"

His expression was bleak. "My siblings and I have been summoned to the lawyer's office tomorrow morning at ten. Something about a letter from our father. Written to me. But the other two are supposed to be there to hear it read aloud. J.B. and Lisette will come with

Mazie and Jonathan, of course. I'd like somebody with *me* who is in my corner."

"It's your family, Hartley. Of course they're in your corner. It wouldn't be appropriate for me to intrude."

"I'm going to have to sit there and let my father berate me from the grave. The others may have forgiven me, but my dad died before I even came home. This isn't going to be pleasant." He pressed three fingers to his forehead as if he had a headache.

She swallowed, feeling frustrated and emotional. Finally, she had worked up the courage to tell Hartley about her pregnancy, and he had rerouted the conversation before she could even start.

"You need to eat," she said. "It will make you feel better." There she went again. Trying to make herself indispensable.

In her small kitchen, she waved him to the table and found him a beer. While she made a second version of the meal she had eaten earlier, Jonathan brooded visibly. His masculinity dwarfed the modest room. Or maybe it was his expansive personality.

Hartley was larger than life. He had the family background and the adventuresome spirit to pull off any scheme he chose to pursue. Go racing off to Europe to uncover a decades-old secret. Buy an enormous wreck of a house and blithely decide to renovate it at a moment's notice.

Sweep a bridesmaid off her feet a year ago and make her fall head over heels in love. That last one was his most outrageous affair. Fiona had been an ordinary woman with an ordinary life until Hartley came along.

She sat beside him and sipped a glass of iced tea while he wolfed down the modest meal. He ate as if he were starving.

It was ridiculous to feel sorry for him. The man had plenty of money. Charleston was chock-full of fabulous restaurants that offered takeout. But she loved him, despite the impossibility of their relationship. She wanted him to be happy.

Suddenly, she knew she couldn't procrastinate any longer. She would make love to him one last time and then lay all her cards on the table. "Hartley," she said. She reached a hand across the table and held his wrist. "Would you like to stay the night?"

* * *

Hartley nearly choked on his soup. His body went on high alert, sensing danger. Is this why he had come? He could have asked Fiona to deliver the painting via local messenger service. He'd told himself the package was too valuable to entrust to other hands.

The truth was far simpler. He had wanted to see Fiona again. Her three-word text had been all the permission he needed.

Even so, he equivocated. "We always end up fighting afterward."

She lifted his hand and kissed his fingers one by one. "Don't be mean, Hartley."

"Would you rather me be *nice*?" He leaned toward her and curled a hand behind her neck, pulling her close for a searing kiss. The taste of her went to his head like 100 proof whiskey.

He had tried to stay away. He really had. But it was a losing battle. Until another man put a ring on her finger, he was going to fight for what he wanted. And he wanted Fee.

Slowly, he stood, tugging her to her feet. After what had happened at the hotel the night of the gala, he was stunned now to realize that

Fiona wanted him as much as he wanted her, not that such a thing was possible.

His body was on fire for her. The hunger consumed him. Something had spooked her when he mentioned *traveling the globe*. He wouldn't make that mistake again. If Fiona was interested in hot and temporary, he would be that guy.

He knew what it felt like to sleep alone. He'd be damned if he would let it happen again. Now that she had offered an olive branch, he was determined to make the most of this extraordinary turn of events.

They navigated the narrow hallway hand in hand. It was still daylight outside. Fiona's bedroom glowed in the late-day sun, even with the curtains drawn. She hadn't made her bed that morning. The tumbled sheets were an erotic invitation.

They barely spoke a word this time. Perhaps because talking always got them in trouble.

He unbuttoned her top. The lacy bra beneath did little to hide pert raspberry nipples. She was softer than he remembered, her breasts fuller and rounder. Maybe absence truly did make the heart grow fonder.

When she was naked, he lifted her into the bed and rapidly removed his own clothes. Climbing in beside her was like coming home.

His breath came in short, jerky gasps. "I won't ask any questions, Fee. Your reasons are your own. But know that I wouldn't want to be any place else in the world right now."

Her lips were bare. Pale pink. Kissable. Wide eyes stared up at him as he leaned over her on one elbow.

She cupped his cheek. "I was afraid you didn't want me anymore."

His rough curse held incredulity. "I'll never stop wanting you, darlin'. You're the one who seems to have a few issues."

When he reached for a condom, she put a hand on his arm. "You won't need that. I took care of things."

"Whatever you say, Fee."

When he moved between her legs and thrust slowly, the sensation of bare skin to bare skin made him shudder. "I've never been with a woman like this. It feels damned incredible."

"Yes," she whispered. She kept her eyes open the entire time, almost as if she were trying to memorize his face.

He gritted his teeth, clenched his jaw. Tried to stave off the climax that was a desperate convergence of condomless sex and long celibate days without her.

Finally, he rolled to his back, taking her with him. Now he could finger her center, send her over the edge. Her orgasm triggered his own. He came forever. Until he was boneless, helpless.

She collapsed on his chest at the end. He held her tightly, stroking her hair. "Fee…"

He trailed off, not knowing what to say and not wanting to cause another argument. Fiona seemed perfectly content when they were together like this. Why was she so skittish in other ways?

At last, she moved away from him and padded in her bare feet to the bathroom. When she returned, she had pulled a T-shirt over her head. It was long enough to cover the tops of her thighs.

Her face glowed with happiness. "It's only eight o'clock. You want to pop popcorn and watch a movie?"

He raised up on his elbows and grinned at her. "Or have sex again?"

"Can't we do both?" She returned his smile with interest.

"Or I could show you the new house."

"You've made progress?"

"A little."

"Sure," she said. "Let me get dressed. You want to walk? The humidity is down. It's a nice evening."

"I could be persuaded."

Fifteen minutes later, they were outside. The scent of bougainvillea and roses mingled with car exhaust and someone cooking a late-evening steak on the grill. The neighborhood was still busy at this hour. Kids on bikes. Grown-ups sitting on front porches, processing the day.

They walked at a leisurely pace. Even so, Hartley's woebegone house was not more than twenty-five minutes away.

He watched Fiona's face as they approached. Her eyes widened. "You've already closed on the property and done all this?"

"I was motivated." And he was trying to use physical exhaustion as a sedative. Being physically close to Fiona when he was here working had taxed his self-control. He took her hand. "Come see the inside."

When he unlocked the front door, a musty smell greeted them. But it wasn't anything as unpleasant as mildew. More of an old-library odor combined with a house shut up in high temperatures.

"Easy," he said as he steered her around piles of rubbish that he had already accumulated. He gave her the grand tour. Parlor. Dining room. Kitchen. An antiquated bathroom. "We can't go upstairs yet. Too dangerous."

She shook her head. "I thought when you went back to work with Jonathan you would hire a contractor."

"I will...eventually. But I needed something to keep me busy in the evenings."

She didn't react at all to his leading comment. In the front hallway, she leaned against the wall and looked up at the cobwebby chandelier. "So are you really going to flip it or live in it? It's awfully big for a guy who says he doesn't want babies."

"Not every man is cut out to be a father."

"I suppose."

Was it his imagination, or did her face look stricken? Maybe she was disappointed in him.

The golden evening lost some of its shine. "We'd better get back," he said gruffly.

He locked up and checked windows. They reversed their route. Fiona had invited him to stay the night. He wasn't sure it was the thing to do. But who was he kidding? He wasn't going to say no.

In the end, they *did* pop popcorn and watch a movie. With his arm around Fiona and her head on his shoulder, it was almost possible to pretend that everything in his life was perfect.

When it was time for bed, the tension escalated almost imperceptibly. This was the first time he had been expressly invited to spend the night. The moment seemed significant, but in light of everything that had happened, he wasn't sure how.

Fiona rounded up a toothbrush for him. They took turns showering and met in the bedroom. She seemed shy. He was torn in a dozen different directions. Tomorrow's visit to the lawyer loomed, though he thrust the knowledge away, determined not to ruin this night. He wanted her badly. Should he disguise his need until she trusted him more?

His beautiful artist made the decision for him. They had barely turned out the light before he felt her hand slide beneath the covers. She wrapped her fingers around his erection. "Make love to me, Hartley."

The sex was perfect. Their bodies knew each other now. He could make her gasp. She knew how to pull him to the edge of release and keep him there until he was ready to cry uncle. They moved together in silent yearning.

As they drifted off to sleep, he was struck by the inescapable notion that tonight was the last time. Sadness enveloped him. Giving up wasn't his style, but he sensed Fiona pulling away. Her thoughts were a mystery.

In fact, she had wanted to talk to him at the hotel, but he had shut her down.

What was the point of being together if all they had was sex? He used to think it was enough, but now he wasn't so sure…

Sixteen

Fiona awoke with a jerk, her heart racing. Someone was in the house. "Hartley…" She whispered his name urgently. When she reached for him, his side of the bed was empty.

Her heart rate slowed, but now she had a bigger worry. Grabbing up her robe, she slipped it over her naked body and belted it. For some reason, she felt the need to tiptoe in her own house.

She found him in the kitchen. He had put on his boxer briefs, but the rest of him was gloriously naked. Ignoring the ache and zing of completely understandable lust in her pelvis, she went to him and combed her fingers through his sleep-rumpled hair. "You want to talk about it?"

He shot her a tired grin, barely enough wattage to even be called a grin. "Not much to say. This is where my color-outside-the-lines behavior catches up with me. I'd just as soon not have witnesses when the lawyer reads this letter from my father, but it seems I'm out of luck."

"I'm sorry."

Hartley shrugged. "It was my choice to go to Switzerland without telling anyone. It was my choice to borrow the money."

"An incredibly large amount of money," she pointed out.

"I thought you were on *my* side."

She kissed his cheek. "I am. And if you want me with you at the lawyer's office, I'll ignore any strange looks I get from your family. But afterward, I really do need to talk to you."

He frowned. "Why can't we talk now?"

Why indeed? She poured herself a cup of orange juice, keeping her back to him as she opened and closed the fridge. "Because it's three in the morning, and I'm not coherent at this hour. Come back to bed."

He took her hand and whirled her around. "Is that an invitation?"

She wrapped her arms around his neck and yawned. "As long as you won't be insulted if I sleep through your manly moves."

He scooped her up and carried her down the hall. "Challenge accepted."

When Fiona awoke the next morning, Hartley was gone, but he had left a note on the pillow beside her.

Had several things to do before the meeting at the lawyer's office. I'll send a car for you around nine thirty. Text me if that's a problem. When we're done there, you and I can find someplace to talk.

You and I can find someplace to talk. Innocuous words for a conversation that would change her life. Her stomach threatened to act up again, but after a cup of hot tea and some preventative saltines, she felt better.

The dress she had worn to the funeral was getting too tight around the waist. Instead, she put on a pair of the nice black pants she had bought recently—the ones with the stretchy elastic waist—and topped them with a sober gray tunic that had three-quarter-length sleeves and decorative black buttons. The dressy top hit her midthigh and disguised her change of shape.

When she added strappy black sandals and black earrings, she looked entirely present-able for an extremely serious legal meeting. She still thought it was a mistake for her to be there.

They were friends and lovers. After she told him her news, even those designations would be gone. As much as she wanted to think every-thing was going to turn out okay, in her heart, she knew the truth.

Today would signal the end of her relation-ship with Hartley Tarleton.

When the driver dropped her off downtown, Hartley was waiting on the sidewalk to greet her. He had showered and shaved and was wearing a suit that was clearly hand tailored. The charcoal-gray fabric emphasized his wide shoulders and his trim waist.

He brushed a kiss against her cheek, but he was distracted.

"You doing okay?" she asked, squeezing his hand.

"I've been better. Let's get this over with."

If any of the Tarleton siblings and their spouses thought it odd for Fiona to be in attendance, they were too well-bred to show it. When Hartley and Fiona joined them in a beautiful reception area, the other four stood and the receptionist ushered them into the lawyer's office.

Here, traditional furnishings reigned. Lots of leather and dark green, navy and burgundy. Was the palette intentional? Meant to impart gravity?

Fiona had always reacted strongly to color and light. Either positively or negatively, the response was a function of her calling.

Today, in this stuffy, overly formal setting, she felt as if the room was trying to smother her. Maybe Hartley felt the same way, because he looked like his tie was too tight, and he was having trouble breathing.

The lawyer wasted no time greeting them. When everyone was seated in a semicircle facing the large mahogany desk, he opened a legal-size folder and shuffled a few papers.

Jonathan leaned forward, frowning. "I don't understand why we're here. I'm my father's executor. There hasn't been time for the death certificate and other initial documents to work their way through the court. Tell us what's going on. Please. What's so urgent about this letter?"

The lawyer was late fifties, early sixties. He was polite, but not warm. His nod was brief. "As you've been told, Gerald Tarleton left a letter to be read in the event of his death. He filed it with my office six months ago. Though it is addressed to Hartley, Mr. Tarleton made it clear that you and your sister were to be here when the contents were revealed."

Mazie frowned as well. "A little too cloak-and-dagger, don't you think? It doesn't sound like my father."

The lawyer bristled. "I assure you, Ms. Vaughan...the letter is entirely legitimate."

Hartley sighed audibly. "We all know what it's going to say." He shot the lawyer a cool stare. "Let's get on with it."

The man nodded. "Very well." He opened a

simple white envelope and extracted a single sheet of paper.

Fiona reached out and gripped Hartley's right hand. His entire body was rigid. This public flogging was cruel, particularly since Jonathan and Hartley had finally begun to mend fences.

When the lawyer stood, she was forced to drag her attention away from Hartley.

The lawyer cleared his throat theatrically.

"My dearest son Hartley:

"If you are reading this letter, it means that I am gone. Though I was very angry with you for leaving and taking the money, in truth, I was angry with myself for my cowardice over the years. I told Jonathan I had written you out of the will, but I did not. I never did. More about that later.

"Some weeks after you disappeared, I discovered you had flown to Europe, and suddenly I understood what was happening in Switzerland. Not the specifics perhaps, but enough to realize that my secret was out.

"I owe all three of you my deepest apologies. I have no excuse other than the fact that I was scared and embarrassed, and I didn't know what to say to all of you now that you were adults.

"I should have done the right thing years ago, but I avoided the pain and let time pass. Now Hartley has to be the one to explain everything.

"Please know that I adored your mother. Losing her nearly wrecked my entire life. I did what I thought I had to do, but I have often wondered if I did all of you a disservice.

"No father could be more proud of his children. Jonathan is the steady hand at the wheel. Hartley has the fire and enthusiasm that propels us all forward. And Mazie, my sweet Mazie, is the heart of the family.

"Whatever you decide about the Vermont situation is up to you. There is no moral high ground. Only regret and sadness.

"Hartley, I addressed this letter to you because I wanted to make absolutely sure you knew that you have never disappointed me. Ever. You have been impulsive at times, but I have come to believe that such impulsiveness is far more admirable than being stuck in endless indecision as I have been.

"Forgive me, son, for letting your brother think ill of you. When I look back at what has happened, I regret that most of all.

"Jonathan will handle the nuts and bolts of dividing the company and the estate. You will all three benefit equally from our collective hard work. Mazie and J.B. have the wonderful house in the historic district. Jonathan and Lisette are building their dream home. To you, Hartley, I leave the beach house. I pray that you will find a partner—a wife—to bring you peace and happiness and many children to carry on your passion for living boldly.

"My plea is that you keep the beach house in the family and that you fill it with joy and laughter and love.

"Goodbye, my dear ones. Please forgive your old father his transgressions and re-member me with fondness.

"Much love to each of you,

"Dad

"(aka Gerald Tarleton)"

* * *

When the lawyer finished reading and tucked the letter away, dead silence reigned for several moments. Hartley was pale, his gaze haunted. Jonathan's grim expression masked a multitude of emotions. Poor Mazie wept bitterly.

The youngest Tarleton offspring wiped her face. "What money? What was he talking about?"

The lawyer stood. "I have another appointment. You're welcome to talk this over here in my office. Stay as long as you like. Goodbye…"

When the man exited, Mazie repeated her question, looking from one brother to the other and back.

Hartley rolled to his feet and paced. "I stole a million bucks from Tarleton Shipping. Jonathan was pissed, and rightly so."

Jonathan groaned audibly. "Damn it, Hartley." His jaw worked. "Tell us what the hell Father was talking about."

Mazie was pale now, too, and trembling. J.B. was none too happy to see his newly pregnant wife upset. "Jonathan is right," he said. "We need to know."

Fiona stood up beside the man who held her

heart. She kissed his cheek. "It's okay," she said. "They can handle it." Then she looked at Jonathan and Mazie. "He didn't want to hurt you. He's kept this terrible secret to himself to spare you pain."

"Tell us now," Jonathan said. "Please."

Fiona nodded, giving the man she loved a reassuring smile. "It's time, Hartley. Let it go."

And so he did. For the next half hour, he talked as if he had been a monk under a vow of silence and finally released. He told them about the blackmail and the hush money and the blackmailer who turned out to be a feeble old man and a relative at that. Then he described the terrible tragedy that happened when they were one and two years old. And about their mother's twin sister. And everything that transpired in the aftermath.

He gave an accounting of everywhere he had been and everything he had done in the past year. He told of the old man's unexpected death and of settling a stranger's estate. He explained that in a storage unit in North Charleston were cartons of family memorabilia none of them had ever seen.

The only thing he *didn't* mention was how

he and Fiona had met and the fact that nine months after that crazy wedding weekend, he had come home for a fleeting visit to tell his family everything. But he chickened out. And instead spent the night with Fiona.

When his incredible tale finally wound to a close, no one spoke for a couple of minutes. Fiona could see on their faces the struggle to accept that a huge part of their lives had been a lie. There were questions, of course. It was a lot to process. Shock made the task more difficult.

Mazie seemed dazed. "So our mother is not our mother…"

Hartley knelt at his sister's feet and took her hands. "I'm so damned sorry, baby girl. You deserved better. We all did."

She shook her head slowly. "But she did care for us while we were growing up."

"I know she did," Hartley admitted. "You have to think, though, she could have injured any one of us or herself there at the end, before Father sent her away. Maybe if she'd had better doctors and treatments early in her life… I don't know. That's why I—"

He stopped suddenly, perhaps realizing at the last moment the insensitivity of explaining to his pregnant sister that he had vowed never to father any biological children of his own.

Jonathan put a hand on Hartley's shoulder, urging him to his feet. When they were eye to eye, Jonathan uttered words that weren't entirely steady. "I'm sorry, Hartley. God knows I can't ever make this up to you. I should have known. I should have trusted you."

Hartley's face finally lightened. "Hell, Jonathan, even Fiona pointed out to me that expecting blind faith from all of you, given the circumstances, was a lot to ask. I'm ready to be done with this. It's consumed over a year of my life. I just want to get back to normal."

Jonathan hugged him tightly. For a long time. When they separated, both men's eyes were suspiciously bright. Jonathan nodded slowly. "I want that, too. This has been an awful day. We're going to be dealing with this for a long time, each in our own way. But we're family. We'll get through it."

Mazie stood up to join her brothers, the three of them standing arm in arm. She kissed each man on the cheek and gave both of them a brilliant smile. "I *hated* knowing the two of you were at odds. I'm so, so grateful I don't have to watch you both being weird anymore."

The laughter that followed smoothed some of the rough edges in the room. High emotions demanded a break, a way to let off steam after the intensity they had shared.

Lisette joined her husband and addressed the group. "You all know that Jonathan and I are still staying at the beach house for now. Why don't we have a cookout on the beach tonight? Hot dogs, roasted marshmallows. We can watch the stars come out. What do you say?"

There was a resounding yes from almost everyone.

Fiona, on the other hand, was painfully aware that her hard times were just beginning. "It sounds wonderful," she said. "I'll come if I can, but I have a couple of things in the works. I'll have to let you know later today."

Mazie was visibly disappointed. "But you'll be at my birthday party, surely."

"I'll do my best."

If her equivocation confused Hartley, he didn't show it. He hugged each member of his family one at a time and then sighed. "Tonight sounds great. But I think we all need time to debrief between now and then. Fiona and I will see you later."

In the general exodus that followed, Fiona didn't correct his assurance. Sooner or later, Hartley's family would realize that he and Fiona had ended their relationship.

Outside in the parking lot, he stretched his neck and loosened his tie. "I'm shot, but I promised you we'd talk, darlin'. Where do you want to go?"

And there it was. The question of the day. She was torn between a need for privacy and the idea that a public place might serve to quell the worst of the storm.

She glanced at her watch. "I think we're late enough to miss most of the lunch crowd. What about that new little place over near Hyman's? I hear they're giving the big kid on the block a run for its money. They have conch fritters I've been wanting to try. And the booths are comfy." Perhaps she was overselling it.

"Sounds good to me." He took off his jacket and tossed it in the back seat of the car. Then he rolled up his sleeves. To Fiona it almost seemed as if he were shedding all the stress and pain and sorrow of the last months. How could she send him back to the depths again?

But how could she continue to lie to the man by omission? How could she not tell him he had fathered a child?

The restaurant's customers, as predicted, had thinned out. Fiona asked for a quiet booth. The hostess took her at her word and seated them in a tight corner in the back of the second floor. When Hartley excused himself to go to the men's room, Fiona slipped the server a twenty and asked the young man to leave them alone once the food came.

Perhaps her face revealed more than she knew. The kid nodded vigorously. "I won't come by at all, unless you wave your glass and want more tea."

"Thanks," Fiona said.

In the end, the food was amazing. It lived up to all the hype and then some. Hartley devoured a platter of clams and oysters and an enormous salad. Fiona nibbled at her fritters and pretended to eat a bowl of seafood bisque.

She was so nervous she was sweating, despite the efficient AC.

As the minutes passed, Hartley's mood rebounded exponentially. "God, I'm glad that's over. Could have been a lot worse."

He took her hand, lifted it and kissed her knuckles. "Thank you, Fee. You saved my life in there."

His crooked male grin was sweet and sexy and affectionate.

"You're welcome," she said. "Your family is strong. I know it was a lot to have dumped on them with no preparation. But they did well. So did you."

She loved him so much it was tearing her apart. She *had* to change his mind. She had to.

As promised, the server had left them alone while they ate. But time was running out. Fiona and Hartley couldn't sit here all afternoon. After a second drink refill and a puzzled frown from the server, Fiona waved him away with an apologetic smile.

Hartley yawned and stretched out his legs under the table. "One of us was up early," he teased.

"You could have waked me to say goodbye."

"Nope," he said cheerfully. "If you'd been awake, I wouldn't have been able to resist making love to you."

His intense stare unnerved her. She knew exactly what he meant. The two of them were like magnets, unable to occupy the same space without touching. "True..." She trailed off, literally sick with nerves.

Hartley stroked the back of her hand. "What did you want to talk about, Fiona? Are you finally going to give in and let me sleep on your sofa?"

When she didn't smile at his joke, he cocked his head. "Fee?" He frowned. "What is it? Why are you so upset? Whatever it is, I'll help you fix it."

Her lower jaw trembled so hard her teeth chattered. "I'm pregnant, Hartley. I'm sorry. It must have been that day you came back from Europe unexpectedly. We were kind of crazy for twenty-four hours. I guess we weren't careful one of those times, or maybe a condom broke. Nothing is a hundred percent. I know you—"

She ground to a halt abruptly, mortified to realize she was babbling.

Hartley hadn't said a word. He was looking at her, but his eyes were blank, his body frozen.

"Say something," she pleaded. "Please."

Every ounce of color drained from his face. She knew her timing was terrible, but she had waited and waited and then the stupid lawyer letter had come. Putting her confession off for a day or a week or a month wasn't going to make this any easier.

She wanted him to yell at her or curse or lose his cool.

Instead, it was as if the man she knew disappeared. In his place was a robot.

Hartley pulled out his wallet, extracted a hundred-dollar bill and tucked it under the sugar container. Then he slid out of the booth, turned his back on her and walked away.

Seventeen

Hartley went to the cookout at the beach. It was the last thing he wanted to do, but he had caused his family too much pain to let them down in such a simple thing.

So he made excuses for Fiona's absence, roasted his hot dog and his marshmallow, and gave a damned fine performance of a man who hadn't a care in the world.

As soon as he could reasonably leave without being rude, he drove back to the city.

He didn't pass Fiona's house. He couldn't bear to go near her street. Instead, he stopped at a sporting-goods store, bought a thick sleeping bag and drove to his newly acquired residence.

Not a residence so much as a dream. A dream of what his life could be with Fiona by his side and all the secrets finally out in the open. He knew now that he was in love with her. Truly, madly, deeply. Probably had been for some time. But last night had been a revelation. Being with her again had been like one of those crazy cartoons where the character gets knocked on the head with a coconut.

His whole outlook had changed.

Even with the lawyer appointment hanging over his head, he'd suddenly known that he could deal with a dead man's letter as long as Fiona was there, too.

What a naive fool he had been. Life was always waiting in the wings to knock a guy on his ass.

His pain and terror were so deep, they consumed him. He'd seen images in Switzerland. Coroner's photographs. Things he would never be able to erase from his brain. Dreadful documentation of a suicide that took so much from so many. He would never ever reveal those pictures to Jonathan or Mazie, never so much as mention them. Even now, he couldn't forget, couldn't get them out of his head. The blood.

So much blood. And his mother's face, pale and perfect in death.

Almost innocent.

He'd seen other photographs, too. That same woman as a child. Laughing. Playing. Carefree. Totally oblivious to the suffering that lay ahead for her.

The transition was horrifying.

Jonathan climbed to the second level, despite the rotting stairs and the broken glass here and there. He flung his pallet on the floor and fell down on his back, his entire body trembling as if he had malaria or some other jungle fever. One moment he was drenched in sweat. The next he wrapped the edges of the sleeping bag around him.

His maternal grandparents had lost two daughters to mental illness. How had they borne the pain? One child was still alive in an institution in Vermont, but she was a shell of herself. After her breakdown, she rarely recognized any of them. She had only fleeting lucid memories of the family she had reared.

Hartley had tried to make his peace with the past by vowing not to perpetuate it. But what now? He had fathered a child. *Sweet Jesus.*

And no use asking if the baby was his. Fiona was as guileless and true as any woman who ever lived. He was the one who had pursued her, bedded her again and again, because he couldn't stay away.

He literally had no idea where to go from here.

Eventually, exhaustion claimed him. He slept in snatches, jerked awake again and again by nightmares. The stuffy house and stark, comfortless bed were no more than he deserved.

He had walked out on Fiona. Hadn't said a word.

How much of an ass could a man be and still consider himself a man?

Toward morning, he splashed water on his face and stared into the mottled mirror in despair. The figure looking back at him was a phantom, a ghost. He had searched his heart for hours on end, even in the midst of sleep.

What should he do? What could he say?

If asking forgiveness was all there was, he might figure that out. But he couldn't go back to Fiona unless he was prepared to talk about the baby. Every time he thought about a child that was his, his blood ran cold in his veins. His brain froze. He was no good to Fiona *or her child*. Couldn't she understand that?

Hunger made him faint. He stumbled going back down the stairs. When he grabbed for the railing, a piece of it splintered, slicing his hand. He stared at the blood dripping from his fingertips.

He was dizzy and weak. For a moment, his dread and pain were so overwhelming, he couldn't see a way forward. Was he like his mother after all?

Fiona had experienced grief many times in her life. Up until now, the worst was a moment long ago when she realized she was too old to be adopted, that she had missed her *window*, that she would never have the family she dreamed about.

She had been luckier than most. Her life had intersected with people who were kind for the most part. There was no memory of abuse to struggle with. No history of alcoholism or drugs. She'd simply been a good kid in an overcrowded governmental system.

Once she was grown, she'd become proud of who she was. She'd created a nest for herself, a niche. Except for brief friendships with a few guys whose faces she barely remembered, she had been content to paint and to draw and to make a living by herself.

She had learned not to dream big dreams, but instead to be satisfied with what she had...who she had become.

Until Hartley Tarleton had burst into her life like a supernova, she believed she *knew* what it was to be content. To be happy.

Like the scene in the *Wizard of Oz* when Dorothy's world morphed from black-and-white into full glorious color, meeting Hartley had shown Fiona feelings and emotions and a whole damned *rainbow* she never knew existed.

Because the climb up the mountain had been so glorious, the fall was brutal. Indescribably agonizing.

She was like two separate women. One exhilarated by the amazing new life she carried. The other crushed by a grief so all encompassing she wanted to hide under the covers.

One day passed. Then two. Then three.

She had believed Hartley would relent. But she had underestimated his pain.

One day bled into the next. She forced herself to eat and exercise and work. Yearning for Hartley was the worst misery she had ever known.

When the one-week mark passed, she knew he wasn't coming. Ever. It became harder to wake up each morning. The only thing that kept her from collapse was knowing she had a responsibility to her child.

It was ten days after the emotional scene in the lawyer's office before she saw Hartley again. By then, she had stopped hoping. She was at work in her studio. When she turned around to get another brush, there he was.

Gaunt and motionless. With a world of agony in his eyes. "I'm sorry," he said gruffly.

She gripped the paintbrush until her knuckles were white. "I didn't need an apology, Hartley. I knew what was going to happen when I told you. I knew it would be bad. I used to imagine scenarios like running away to join the circus. Or taking a different name and starting a new life on the other side of the country. No matter how hard I tried, I couldn't find a way around the obvious. A woman has to tell a man when he has a baby on the way. It's a moral obligation."

Hartley stared at her bleakly. His eyes were almost black in this light. "I'm sorry I made things terrible for you," he said. "You must have been so scared." He stood with his hands in his pockets. His jeans were ancient and torn, not at all the look of a wealthy man, one of Charleston's elite. The navy T-shirt was equally old and stained. Clearly, he had been working on the house he had bought.

"I *was* scared," she said quietly. "But you can't help your feelings. I knew the baby thing wasn't a whim. You were frightened. And rightly so."

He dropped his chin to his chest for a moment and sighed deeply. When he finally lifted his head and tried to smile, it was almost too painful to witness. "I couldn't deal with the news at first," he said. "I knew an apology was worthless until I was willing to talk about the baby."

"And now?"

He swallowed. "I didn't tell you everything. I didn't tell Mazie or Jonathan either."

Her stomach clenched. What more could there be? "Tell me what?" she asked softly.

"My uncle showed me the coroner's photographs. A crime scene. Bloody. Horrifying.

Our mother, the woman none of us remember, looked so peaceful and beautiful. But she was dead. By her own hand. And then he showed me pictures from her childhood. A tiny little girl laughing…playing with puppies. A six-year-old wearing a tutu and beaming. The juxtaposition of those pictures was almost incomprehensible. That's when I knew I couldn't bear to father a child. How could I watch him or her grow up, never knowing if the illness that stole my mother lingered beneath the surface?"

Fiona trembled. "All life is a risk, Hartley. None of us can see the future. Some lives are cut short at eighteen. Others stretch out to ninety or a hundred years." Hot tears sprang to her eyes and rolled down her cheeks. She cried the tears he couldn't shed, grieving, lost.

At last, he approached her, perhaps moved by her distress. "Let's go to the living room," he said. "You look exhausted."

Hand in hand they walked down the hall. Simply being with him again was more than she had hoped for, but they were a long way from any kind of resolution.

Hartley released her and sat on one end of the sofa. Did he think she would maintain some kind of distance between them? Not a chance in hell. He was here. With her. She would fight for their happiness.

She curled up beside him and leaned her head on his shoulder. He took her hand in his. The silence was not quite peaceful, but it held gratitude, at least on her part.

She sifted through the words she wanted to say, but ultimately, the decision would have to be Hartley's. "Here's the thing," she said, praying for some kind of divine guidance. "When I was a child, six or seven years old, I lived in an orphanage. It was a nice place. Clean. Safe. But the one thing they couldn't take away was my loneliness. It lived in my bones. I painted a life in my imagination, a life I wanted so very badly. The reality was different."

He grimaced. "It hurts me to think of you like that."

"There came a time when I had to let go of my fantasies and accept that my life couldn't be the imaginary one I craved. But it could be good."

"How did you get there? How did you give up the wanting and the needing and the disappointment?"

She straightened and faced him, her legs crisscrossed. "You'll laugh. It had to do with ice cream."

He blinked. "Ice cream?"

"Yes. For whatever reason, one of the dairies in the area decided to donate ice cream to the orphanage. Every Friday at 3 p.m., a truck would roll up in the driveway, and a big carton packed in dry ice was off-loaded, filled with orange sherbet push-pops."

"I loved those," he said, his smile more genuine this time.

"I still do. In fact, if I see a kid in my neighborhood eating one on the sidewalk, it takes me back to those warm, perfect afternoons."

"I don't understand how ice cream healed your existential crisis."

She chuckled. "Well, first of all, I hadn't a clue that I was having a crisis, existential or otherwise. All I knew was that I was sad. Yet somehow, when I tasted that treat, my sadness went away for a little while. I began to understand that if something as good as orange sherbet push-pops existed in life, then somehow, someday, I was going to be okay."

"That's pretty deep for a kid so young."

Fiona shrugged. "What can I say? I was a wise old soul."

He kissed her temple. "Some of us are more hardheaded than others. I didn't want to see you again, Fee, until I dealt with my mother. I couldn't let her story define mine."

"And now?" She wanted to hold him and kiss him, but this moment was too important. Hope and fear duked it out in her chest. Right now, hope was winning. Barely.

"I adore you, Fiona James. And I won't live in fear," he said firmly. "What happened in the past was a tragedy. My child, our child, may struggle with any number of serious problems. Or maybe he or she will float through life as one of the lucky ones. Either way, I'm going to love you and this baby for the rest of my life."

"Truly?" Her chin wobbled.

He kissed her nose. "Truly. Marry me, Fee. Big wedding. Small one. I don't care. But I don't want to wait."

"Me either." She took his hand and placed it on her slightly rounded tummy. "I've already picked out your wedding gift. It's the only thing

I could think of for the man who has everything."

He flattened his hand against her belly, pressing gently, his expression transfixed. "The pregnancy is good? And you? The baby?"

"We're fine. Better than fine." She cupped his face in her hands. "I want you to make love to me, Hartley. I've missed you so much. It's been an eternity since I felt you next to me, skin to skin, heart to heart."

He tugged her to her feet. "I've never had sex with a pregnant woman." The look in his eyes told her he liked the idea.

"Sure you have," she said, laughing. "You just didn't know it."

In her bedroom, they stood on either side of the bed and stared at each other. When they met in the center of the mattress, kneeling, he brushed the hair from her face, his gaze searching. "No more looking back, my sweet Fee. I swear it. From now on, I'll be under your feet at every turn. You'll never be lonely as long as I have breath in my body."

"I love you, Hartley."

"Not as much as I love you."

He kissed her then, a kiss that started out

with relief and thanksgiving for having weathered the storm, but ended up in the same fiery passion that bound them at every turn.

Clothes flew in four directions. Bare skin met bare skin. He entered her carefully, as though she were a fragile china doll.

She clutched his warm muscled shoulders, her breath coming faster, her body arching into his. "I won't break, silly man."

"No, you won't," he said, burying his face in the curve of her neck. "Because if you ever fall, I'll be there to catch you."

"You're mine," she whispered.

"Orange sherbet push-pops, darlin'. For both of us. From now on. I found you, Fee. Against all odds. I'll never let you go."

Then he gave up on words, and showed her that some happiness was even better than ice cream…

Five days later…

"Be careful. Don't tear the paper." Fiona fretted as she and Hartley climbed the steps of J.B. and Mazie's classic home. J.B. had invited half of Charleston for Mazie's kick-ass party.

But first the family was gathering to give her their gifts.

Over punch and cookies and with much laughter and teasing, paper and ribbon fluttered through the air. Lisette and Jonathan had ordered a handmade French baby doll for the woman who had grown up far too soon.

Mazie traced the doll's lifelike lashes and smiled through her tears. "I love it."

Everyone smiled. Then Hartley handed over the next gift. "This is from Fiona and me. Open with care."

Mazie's astonishment when she saw the wedding-day photograph immortalized in oils warmed Fiona's heart. "Hartley commissioned the gift," she said. "It was his idea."

Mazie screeched and hugged them both. "It's incredible," she cried.

Lisette and Mazie looked at each other and smiled. Lisette took Mazie's hand, and they stepped in front of the birthday girl. Lisette took a deep breath. "There's one more present, Mazie. But you'll have to wait a bit for this one."

Fiona nodded. "We didn't want your little one to grow up alone, so Lizzy and I are giving you two cousins, maybe even a birthing room for three if the timing is right."

Mazie's eyes rounded. "Are you serious?"

Hartley studied the pandemonium that followed with a full heart and a happy grin.

Jonathan and J.B. moved to flank him. "We're toast, aren't we?" Jonathan said. "Three pregnant wives? Whew..."

J.B. nodded. "We'll be wrapped around their little fingers. At their beck and call."

Hartley blew a kiss to his precious bride-to-be. "Any complaints, gentlemen?"

The other two shook their heads ruefully. "Not a one," they said in unison.

Hartley felt the world click into sharp focus as joy bubbled in his veins like fine champagne. Today was a new life, a new start. He was a damned lucky man...

* * * * *

LET'S TALK

Romance

For exclusive extracts, competitions
and special offers, find us online:

- **f** facebook.com/millsandboon
- ⊙ @millsandboonuk
- 🐦 @millsandboon

Or get in touch on 0844 844 1351*

For all the latest titles coming soon,
visit millsandboon.co.uk/nextmonth

Want even more
ROMANCE?

Join our bookclub today!

'Mills & Boon books, the perfect way to escape for an hour or so.'

Miss W. Dyer

'Excellent service, promptly delivered and very good subscription choices.'

Miss A. Pearson

'You get fantastic special offers and the chance to get books before they hit the shops'

Mrs V. Hall

Visit millsandbook.co.uk/Bookclub and save on brand new books.

MILLS & BOON